TO TH

Also in Arrow by Peter Spence

Some of our Best Friends are Animals
To the Manor Born (Book 1)

To the Manor Born

Book 2

PETER SPENCE

Arrow Books

Arrow Books Limited
17–21 Conway Street, London W1P 6JD

An imprint of the Hutchinson Publishing Group

London Melbourne Sydney Auckland
Johannesburg and agencies
throughout the world

First published 1980
Reprinted before publication and 1981

Set in Plantin by A-Line Services, Saffron Walden, Essex

Made and printed in Great Britain
by The Anchor Press Ltd, Tiptree, Essex

ISBN 0 09 923440 8

1

If there is one thing worse than spending Christmas with cousins, in-laws, aunts, uncles, nieces and nephews, it is spending Christmas without them.

Now, for the first time in her life, this was to be the fate of Audrey fforbes-Hamilton. One Christmas the manor was full of people, echoing with the sound of squabbles and breaking toys, and all the excruciating atmospherics of a family Christmas – and the next, it was all gone – even the house.

That is not to say that Grantleigh Manor was no longer standing – in fact, it might have made life easier for her if it weren't. For there it stood outside the lodge window as an enduring monument to halcyon days, a golden age from which the gilt continued to flake.

Audrey was in one of her 'how are the mighty fallen' moods which, when the thought of Richard DeVere and his mother usurping the ancient family right to the estate entered her head, became a 'how are the humble exalted' feeling.

Many moons had waxed and waned since usurper and usurped had been momentarily reconciled in a dark country lane near Harborough on the way back from the lord lieutenant's charity gala. Viewed in the cold light of day, the incident embarrassed them both. It had been an untimely declaration of kindred feeling, of emotions which their respective backgrounds in normal circumstances had guarded them against. But these had been no normal circumstances – a flare-up born of panic – each was faced with the prospect of losing the other for ever. To all intents and purposes, of which both had many, it served no practical purpose whatever.

It didn't alter the fact that their respective attitudes towards Grantleigh Manor, and all it stood for, were incompatible. They both regretted the compromises they had made that evening and pretended it had never happened. They retrenched – they did not communicate for a while. There was plenty of time.

But now it was Christmas – a season which called for goodwill towards men – a category from which it was difficult to exclude each other. Indeed, they both looked forward to Christmas as a time they could safely resume contact, but under the cover of the festival's social protocol.

DeVere was anxious that, when he next met Audrey, it would not be to receive a dressing down about some trifling neglect of his duties as lord of the manor. He made a particular point of finding out what went on in the Christmases before his encumbency, and saw to it that there was no break in the continuity of tradition. He did it to please Audrey, but in doing so, he made a mistake.

Christmas Day fell on a Tuesday – an accident which could be relied upon to bring the country to a halt for a fortnight. But there would be no let up for Audrey. For weeks she had already busied herself with the normal Christmas activities on the estate – the collection for the old people, the carol singing, ordering the flowers for the church, the holly picking, the children's party, the staff knees-up, the yuletide log-burning – and she engaged in a burst of charitable activity on behalf of those she blanketed under the heading, 'less fortunate'.

Until now, Audrey hadn't begun to consider herself in that category, yet if the reality of her new situation were allowed to sink in – with its attendant poverty and plummet of living standards – she was certainly less fortunate than she had been at the same time last year. But she was schooled in self-negation for the public good, and even when a gift parcel designated for the poor and needy was delivered on her own doorstep by the rector, she didn't let it get to her. That is, until church service the Sunday before Christmas.

She didn't mind working herself to the bone and being generous with her time and resources when she had neither the means nor the spirit to do so, but to hear somebody else getting the credit was more than she could bear. And that was what was happening now. The rector was brazenly thanking DeVere from the pulpit for all his good work; admittedly, he had instigated the activity, but who had actually done the work? Audrey fforbes-Hamilton, that's who. What's more, DeVere seemed quite prepared to accept the rector's blandishments as he sat in the church in the old fforbes-Hamilton family pew. (And *that* was another thing!)

'The Christmas collection for old people of the parish,' the rector was intoning, 'raised the sum of four hundred pounds. A record amount, due to a substantial contribution from our lord of the manor, Mr DeVere. Our thanks are due to him.'

If looks could kill, both the rector and DeVere should then have dropped dead. Audrey's scowl left them in no doubt that, in her view, our thanks were due to her.

'Then last night we had the staff party and I gather a good time was had by all.'

In the rear pews, the white faces which masked the sore heads of the estate staff – or the Mideonites as Audrey always called them – bore testimony to the rector's observation.

'And our thanks must go to all those who worked so hard to make it a success. Especially' – Audrey preened herself hopefully – 'to Mr DeVere, our lord of the manor.'

Audrey did what she always did when in distress. She turned to Marjory, her neighbour and school friend who was sitting next to her.

'It was me – me,' she mouthed in considerable anguish.

She looked across the aisle to where Richard DeVere sat with his mother, as the rector continued his citation.

'Now, tomorrow being Christmas Eve, we shall make the church ready for our candlelight procession, and the blessing of the crib at the midnight service. In the afternoon, the women will be decorating the church . . .'

Audrey squirmed. If that was a reference to her, she resented being referred to as 'the women'.

'. . . and I gather that we can expect an even better display than usual, owing to another generous donation from Mr DeVere, our lord.'

The thought of DeVere's new-found divinity sent another shiver through Audrey, as the rector turned towards the altar and mumbled a string of garbled syllables which the congregation knew to be:

'May the words of my mouth and the meditations of all our hearts be now and always acceptable in Thy sight, O Lord, our strength and our Redeemer.' Indeed they may, but there remained those here on earth in whose sight they had not been acceptable.

'When it's Mr DeVere this, and our lord that, well, something is rotten in the state of Denmark,' moaned Audrey, when she and Marjory were back at the lodge.

'I thought he came from Czechoslovakia,' said Marjory.

'So he may,' replied Audrey. 'But the point is, the rector didn't utter one word about all my hard work. This year I was just "the women". "The women" will decorate the church – not even "the ladies" will decorate the church.'

'But you are going to do it, though, aren't you?'

'Of course. Well, me and "the women". But I've got a jolly good mind not to.'

Having a 'jolly good mind not to' was no reason in Audrey's rubric not to observe ancient tradition. Besides, she had already made a start, rallying her cohorts to gather what flowers and foliage they could, and she had told Brabinger, her trusted butler, to bring the church crib down from the attic.

Brabinger, too, was possessed of the Christmas spirit and did not regard the restrictive confines to the lodge as any obstacle to the celebration of Christmas in the grand manner of previous years. While his mistress was in church, he had been in the drawing room working on a little Christmas refinement of his own devising. He had been busy fixing the fairy lights on to the Christmas tree and was just about to fit his homemade attachment which made them blink when he heard her return.

'Brabinger, what on earth are you doing?' demanded Audrey, as she strode into the darkened room.

'I'm preparing a little surprise for you, madam,' stammered Brabinger.

'In the dark?'

'They look better in the dark, madam.'

'What do?'

'Fairy lights, madam.'

He switched them on.

'Oh, how lovely, Brabinger.'

'There's more,' said the old retainer with enthusiasm. 'Do you remember how the lights on the big trees at the manor used to blink?'

'Yes,' said Audrey cautiously, remembering the débâcle when he brought the bell-box system over from the manor. He plugged in his circuit breaker.

'I've made a little device which makes them go off and come on again every three seconds,' said the inventor proudly. He switched on.

There was a rapid sequence of explosions as each coloured light bulb took its turn to blow. A cloud of smoke issued from the transformer and the smell of burning plastic and rubber pervaded the room.

'Well?' said Audrey unmoved, but with anticipation.

'Well, what, madam?'

'I thought you said they come on again.'

'Teething troubles,' he reassured her.

But Audrey needed more assurance when it came to Brabinger's electrical expertise.

'Now, I think we can learn to live without your little belisha beacon,' Audrey counselled sternly. 'In fact, I forbid you to mess with the wiring in this house ever again.'

Brabinger was disconsolate.

'Now, let's have some light on the subject,' Audrey said with an air of finality.

Marjory switched on the lights.

'No, draw the curtains,' commanded Audrey, striding to the window. 'It's cheaper.'

She threw back the curtains, letting in both the light and that view of the ever-present reminder of the good old days in the shape of the manor. But it was not the sight of the grand old building which reminded her that her life was disintegrating. It was the bird table on her terrace. Its supporting pole was standing sound enough, but the plinth it supported, with its little wooden pillars and its thatched roof, were hanging off it at what, in the jargon of sailors' hats, is known as 'a jaunty angle'.

'How did the bird table get like that, Brabinger?'

'I can't think, madam,' said Brabinger, coiling a flex around his hand as he packed his technological dreams away. 'I did see a robin on it this morning.'

'What on earth was it doing?'

'Fighting off one of the farm cats, madam.'

'Well, if you want something constructive to do, you can mend that. Now, where's the crib?'

'The crib, madam?' said Brabinger, as if it was the first he'd heard of it.

'You were supposed to be looking for a crib.'

'Oh, yes. I did look for it in the attic, madam, but I didn't manage to find it.'

'Glory,' sighed Audrey. 'That's all I need.'

'What's wrong?' asked Marjory, seeing her sudden distress.

'I thought the crib would have come over from the manor with everything else,' Audrey grumbled. 'But if it isn't in the attic, it means *he's* got it.'

'Who?'

'Our lord.'

'That's good, isn't it?' said Marjory. 'It means that he'll have to do the crib.'

Audrey rounded on her.

'Good?' she huffed. 'Good! It means that he'll be taking over my one remaining Christmas duty, and that I can't have.' Her irritation abated. 'Anyway,' she added calmly with a scheming glint in her eye, 'if it's at the manor, I know where it is, and he'll never find it.'

But his mother already had. Mrs Polouvička had been down in the laundry room, below the old kitchens which were now never used. She had taken to going for long walks in the afternoon, many of which did not even take her out of the house. Rather than face the cold winter winds which swept through the valley, she contented herself with exploring the house, space enough for all the exercise she needed.

Although its nethermost extremities were now unserviceable, it had not always been so, and the old lady had developed a keen interest in the original function of every room. She enjoyed imagining what it must have been like to live in the house when every room was fully functional and serving the purpose for which it was built. It was on one of these excursions that she had seen a box in one of the partitions of an old washing tub. And when the rector happened to call in just before Christmas, the mention of the crib for the church put her in mind of it.

'The crib has always been provided by the manor,' the vicar had remarked, and within minutes there was a box of crib figures between them, and DeVere and the old lady were taking them out, one by one. And horrified they were at the dilapidated condition of them.

'One headless shepherd.'

'One three-legged donkcy.'

'One wingless arch-angel.'

'One camel, less hump.'

'One hump, less camel.'

'One wise man bearing gifts – a donkey's leg by the look of it.'

'It looks like the mice have been at it,' said DeVere despairing that anything as tatty as this could have been harboured under his roof.

'I'm sure it's not beyond your powers to patch it up,' said the rector.

'I'm not one of the world's patchers,' declared DeVere piously. His mother was more practical.

'We have to have a crib by tomorrow afternoon,' she reminded him.

'And have it, we shall,' promised DeVere, going to the phone. 'I have influence in high places.'

'But not that high,' said his mother, looking heavenwards.

'God, no.'

The rector coughed, embarrassed by the blasphemy.

'No relation,' DeVere assured him, going to the phone. 'I'll have a crib sent down. I remember ordering a gross of them last July for our Christmas window display. Saw one in a window last week. Just the thing.'

He dialled a number, and a voice crackled at the other end of the phone.

'Head office, here,' said DeVere. 'Get me window dressing, please.'

The thought of the crib languishing in the bowels of the manor disturbed Audrey.

'If he finds out he's sitting on something I want, he'll make an issue out of it,' she confided to Marjory. 'So we'll just have to find another crib.'

'Where?' Marjory asked practically. 'I mean, it's Christmas Eve tomorrow.'

'All right, then,' said Audrey, without a moment's hesitation. 'We'll just have to make one.'

Once decided by Audrey, a thing was as good as done. Within seconds the construction of the new crib was organized.

'Brabinger can make the stable, and you can make the animals, Marjory,' Audrey suggested. 'That seems to be in character.'

'And what are you going to make?'

'The mother and child, of course.'

'You couldn't do that to save your life.'

'On the contrary, I'm very clever with my hands. I was the Rodin of the lower remove. Remember?'

'How do I make the animals?'

'You made some very nice animals for that WI competition.'

This contest they both remembered, mainly for being a welcome change from competitive jam and cake making and gardens on plates; on this occasion they had had to make an animal out of a vegetable.

'I seem to remember I won with a giraffe made out of carrots,' Audrey recalled. 'It was patently obvious that I was the one with the most skill and imagination.'

'You were also the judge,' Marjory reminded her.

'I know. How do you think your frogs made out of a marrow came second?'

'Well, frogs are all wrong for this,' said Marjory. 'There's nothing in the Bible about shepherds abiding in the fields keeping watch over their frogs by night – and no giraffes either. That's Noah's ark.'

Brabinger came into the room bearing a salver with a letter on it.

'Ah, Brabinger,' said Audrey as she took the envelope and began to open it. 'We're going to make a Christmas crib. Do you think you could make a stable?'

'Well, I was always rather good at making model aeroplanes,' the old man boasted.

'Just a stable, not a Sopwith camel.'

'What do I make it out of, madam?'

'Anything you can find. Adopt, adapt, improve.'

Audrey looked at the envelope.

'Oh, it's a Christmas card from our lord.'

'Who?'

'Mr DeVere. The almighty Mr DeVere.'

She looked at the design of the card.

'Though what an artist's impression of his new Brent Cross retail outlet has to do with Christmas, I cannot think.' She read out the inscription.

'Happy *X*mas to all our customers,' and cringed.

'It's Christmas, not Xmas. Makes it sound like a skin complaint.' She opened it up and a note fell out. It was an invitation for Audrey to go to the manor and have Christmas dinner with DeVere and his mother. She read the wording of the invitation aloud without emotion, then slowly crumpled the note up and threw it in the fire.

'Aren't you going then?' said Marjory.

'Certainly not.'

'Are you sure?'

'Of course I'm sure. How do you think I'd feel up at the manor surrounded by so many reminders of the good old days? You're forgetting that it was only a year ago that the whole family was there.'

She sighed.

'We had such a wonderful time.'

'Yes, I know. I was there.'

'It was one of the best Christmases we'd ever had – playing Sardines all over the house after lunch, coming in exhausted after the Boxing Day hunt and watching Basil Brush.'

Marjory took up the chorus.

'Pulling crackers, and Marton haranguing us on the state of British industry.'

'Yes, just because his Chinese puzzle was made in Hong Kong.'

The two friends laughed. Brabinger smiled – he was not paid to laugh. Audrey turned solemn for a moment.

'No, I couldn't possibly go to the manor this year.' She instructed Brabinger to telephone the manor and turn down the invitation.

'Should I give a reason, madam?'

'Yes, you can say I have a previous engagement.'

Brabinger left the room to see to it.

'Have you really got a previous engagement?' Marjory asked when he had gone.

'Yes, of course I have. With you. You always spend Christmas Day with me.'

Marjory looked away with embarrassment, as if possessed of a guilty secret.

'Well, times change. I can't imagine it this year,' she ventured bravely.

Audrey was horrified.

'Why not?'

'A previous engagement.'

'Don't be ridiculous, Marjory. You never have a previous engagement.'

'Well, I have this year.'

'Where?'

'Up at the manor, if you must know – with Mr DeVere.'

This came as a bombshell to Audrey.

'You mean you are going to spend Christmas Day with Mr DeVere?' she exploded.

'Yes, he asked me.'

'Well, that's no reason for accepting.'

'Just because you don't want to spend Christmas Day with Richard, it doesn't mean . . .'

'Oh, it's Richard now, is it?' Audrey interrupted heatedly.

'You know very well he likes us to use his Christian name.'

'Christian name, huh,' Audrey snorted, breathing metaphorical fire. 'The nearest he gets to Christianity is stirring his coffee with an apostle teaspoon. And what's more, in church he had his eyes open right the way through the blessing.'

'Oh, and how would you know that, if yours weren't?'

Marjory was determined to stand her ground.

'I do think you might be a bit more complimentary about him. After all, it is Christmas, and he is doing his stuff.'

'Only to salve his conscience over making a fortune out of his supermarkets. Christmas to him is just an excuse to get a lot of people to buy a lot of things they can't afford which people they don't like don't want.'

'I think you're being beastly about him. After all, if you're going to be alone on Christmas Day, you've only got yourself to blame.'

The prospect of being alone on Christmas Day now occurred to Audrey for the first time. She dwelt on this horror for a moment.

'Possibly,' she said. 'All the same, one did think one's best friend would support one – especially at Christmas,' she added, trying to conceal her self pity.

'It's no good your trying to make me feel guilty.'

'I wouldn't dream of it,' Audrey lied. 'It will be on Christmas Day that the full implications of my new situation will come home to me. Spending it alone as I shall have to do, without undue trauma, will be a feat of moral courage which will keep me going for the rest of the year.'

Nothing like a bit of tear-jerking rhetoric to stir Marjory's compassion. It had worked so many times before.

'I shall resign myself to a very boring Christmas here all by myself,' Audrey declaimed theatrically.

Here she looked out of the window longingly towards the manor with her back to Marjory, and left a long pause which shamed Marjory into breaking the silence.

'Oh, all right,' she capitulated. 'I'll come to you for Christmas.'

'Good. That's settled then,' said Audrey, cheerfully, snapping out of her doleful sham. 'Now, you run along home and be back here in the morning with your oxes and your asses.'

'Made out of vegetables?'

'No, save them. But bring them anyway and we'll have them for Christmas lunch.'

By the following afternoon Audrey had transformed a set of fat table candles into a plausible set of crib figures – mother and child, a Joseph and a couple of shepherds – with the aid of a lighted taper and an old Girl Guide penknife. She still had a few days in which to get the wise men ready for Epiphany. Meanwhile, Brabinger had been busy in the kitchen working away at his stable.

'There. What do you think of that?' said Audrey. 'The holy family.' She lined the figures up for inspection.

'Yes, madam,' admired Brabinger, clutching his stable under his arm. 'After Michelangelo?' he complimented.

'No, Brabinger. They were long *before* Michelangelo. Now, let's see yours.'

Brabinger placed his stable on the table. It was a firmly constructed edifice, set on a plinth with a thatched roof.

'Excellent,' beamed Audrey. 'Who said we couldn't knock up a crib if we put our minds to it? Let's put the figures in and see how they look.'

Easier said than done. She took Joseph and tried to put him through the stable door, but he and the stable were built to a different scale. Either his head or his feet would have to go, if he were going to fit.

'Oh dear,' said Brabinger, 'it would appear you've made your figures too big, madam.'

'You mean you've made your stable too small,' she contradicted.

Brabinger knew his place. 'Of course, madam. Slip of the tongue. But you didn't specify any particular size.'

'I left that to your intelligence. I knew that was a great risk, but I didn't know you were going to make something the size of a bird table.'

The bird table reference was intended as an image, not the statement of fact which suddenly dawned on her. She scrutinised the structure again with a feeling of *déjà vu*, and glanced through the french window to the terrace. There, just as she feared, stood a pole supporting the empty space where a bird table once had been.

'Brabinger, how could you?' she admonished.

'"Adopt, adapt, and improve", that's what you said, madam,' faltered Brabinger.

'Yes, but I said nothing about destroy. It's too small, anyway. You'll just have to make a bigger one.'

Brabinger turned and left the room sorrowfully.

'And if I find Bertie's kennel missing in the morning, there'll be trouble,' she called after him.

But her troubles were not yet over. Not by a long chalk. Within a few minutes, Marjory was in the room submitting her handiwork. She admired the stable and the holy family.

'Oh, aren't they lovely?' gushed Marjory.

'Thank you, Marjory,' acknowledged Audrey graciously.

'Just one thing, though,' Marjory added, 'haven't you made them too small?'

Audrey stiffened.

'Oh, so too small now, are they?'

'Well, look at these.' Marjory delved into her bag and produced a felt donkey and a few fluffy cows and sheep.

There was nothing wrong with them independently, for they were good replicas, except in one respect. They were each of them twice the size of the stable, let alone Audrey's figures. Audrey was furious and stared at them speechless.

'You didn't say anything about size,' insisted Marjory.

'Well, I have now – *my* size.'

'I suppose my sheep and donkey could go outside the stable.'

'They'd merely look silly, Marjory. Besides, that donkey just isn't up to snuff. So it's back to the drawing board.'

She took a closer look at the donkey and held it up.

'Mary was supposed to have come all the way from Nazareth on this. This one wouldn't have got her further than the end of the drive.'

By the following afternoon, some semblance of a compromise had been achieved, concessions having been made by Brabinger, who enlarged his stable, and by Marjory who shrank her animals. The adjustments and haste occasioned a fall in their standards of workmanship. Brabinger simply ran out of wood and patched up the holes in the fabric with whatever came to hand, which included a biscuit tin lid for the one wall, and old bootlaces for the thatch.

As for Marjory, she had been forced to give her animals much thinner limbs, which meant that she could not get enough stuffing down the legs to offer the body any support. The donkey just sank down on to its stomach with its legs splayed out and her cows' back legs buckled under the weight of the udders so that they sat upright on their rumps like circus poodles. Audrey's holy family – the candle-grease figures – were already beginning to melt in the heat of the room and heads were beginning to loll.

But the three of them were so proud of the achievement of having got a crib made at all that they were blinded to its patent flaws. They had no preconception of how their masterpiece would be received when it went on public view, so they thought that the sniggers which it evinced from the flower-women in the church when they delivered it must have been occasioned by some private joke of their own.

It was getting dark when they arrived at the church to find the decorations well under way. Audrey ordered Brabinger into the vestry to switch on the nave lights. It was not a particularly complicated switchboard, but an electrician of Brabinger's incompetence was quite capable of first switching the central heating off and the organ on before his haphazard stabbing at the console had the required result.

'You see, Marjory,' said Audrey despairingly, 'he can't even turn a simple switch.'

The light that now shone in darkness was not altogether welcome for it revealed a horror which Audrey had not anticipated. As she came forward to set her masterpiece on the cleared literature table under the pulpit – the traditional position of the crib – she found it already occupied. There was a crib already there – a spanking new one with huge and intricately detailed figures painted in gaudy colours. Inside the stable, bathed in a theatrical glow of purple lights, was composed an exquisitely carved holy family, surrounded by lifelike shepherds and perfectly formed livestock. Beyond were the flat rooftops of a Bethlehem townscape, against a spangled backdrop of a starry sky which hung in the distance, sparkling like a magician's tablecloth. In short, it was ghastly.

'What on earth?' exclaimed Audrey. 'Marjory, come and look at this.'

Marjory bustled up behind her.

'Oh, how divine,' she gasped.

Audrey became stern.

'It is anything but divine. It's common and vulgar and new. Brabinger, put that down and come and help me get this monstrosity out of the way.'

They were just about to shift this newly installed abomination, when its donor walked down the aisle.

'Oh, good, it's arrived,' said DeVere expecting gratitude.

'So this is your work, is it?' said Audrey.

'I arranged it, yes.'

'I might have guessed.'

'Rather snazzy, don't you think? The rector told me the crib was always provided by the manor, so – eh, *voilà*!'

'Not by the manor,' argued Audrey. 'By *me*. The crib has been provided by me ever since I can remember, and before that, by my family since . . .'

'Yes, yes,' interrupted DeVere, who'd heard this all before, 'since the year two thousand BC.'

'Don't be ridiculous. They didn't have cribs in two thousand BC.' Marjory giggled as Audrey went on, 'The point is that, by tradition, I do the crib every year and, at a cost of considerable time and effort, a crib I have done.' With an expansive gesture she drew DeVere's attention to her masterpiece.

DeVere roared with laughter. 'Oh, I think we can do better than that, don't you?' He turned his attention to his own offering. 'Wait until you've seen this in its full glory,' he said, going round the back of the crib and flicking a switch. The nativity scene lit up, and the backdrop burst into life. The stars began to shine, then, as a dawn sun rose over the horizon, they faded and gave way to a bright daylight sky. This was followed in sequence by a twilight effect in which the sun set in a blaze of colour, the moon rose and the stars once more began to twinkle as the sky darkened with nightfall.

It was quite dreadful, and its effect was not improved by a plunky rendering of 'Jingle Bells' which accompanied the garish tableau. It took about thirty seconds for the full sequence to go through.

'At the proper speed it does that cycle every twenty minutes,' said DeVere with the enthusiasm of a small boy with a new toy. Brabinger applauded.

'Most ingenious, if I may say so, sir.'

'No, you may not say so,' said Audrey.

'He's right you know, Audrey,' DeVere judged. 'People stood in Oxford Street watching for hours for that.'

'In Oxford Street? You mean you used the Christmas story to pull crowds?'

'It was in one of the windows of one of my stores, yes,' DeVere stated without apology. 'So when the rector told us we were expected to provide a crib . . .'

'A crib, yes, not a planetarium. I suppose it has nodding donkeys as well, with eyes that light up every half-hour?'

But DeVere wasn't listening. He was round the back of the machine hunting for something.

'There should be a guiding star somewhere,' he said. He traced a length of loose flex until he came to a star-shaped piece of perspex, about nine inches in diameter, with a yellow bulb behind it.

He held it up and, trailing the flex, walked away from the crib, and hooked it on to some holly on the front of the pulpit. He pressed a button on the crib base, and it came on – though not to his satisfaction.

'It's supposed to twinkle,' he said with disappointment.

'Richard, this is supposed to be Bethlehem. You're making it look like Tokyo high street. Why don't you go the whole hog and have a neon sign saying "DeVere's Pork Pies"?'

He ignored the barb.

'They haven't sent the transformer,' he said, looking around for a missing accessory.

This sounded a chord of familiarity in Audrey's memory.

'What did you say?' she asked.

'There's no circuit breaker. It's supposed to make the star twinkle,' he replied still searching.

'Oh, one of those,' said Audrey knowingly. 'Brabinger, has one of those, haven't you?' she added, turning to the butler, who was still gazing in wonder at the crib. He had to be startled out of his reverie.

'Yes, madam, but you did say I wasn't to play with electricity.'

Audrey ignored his protest.

'Go and get it.'

'Are you sure, madam?'

'Yes, of course I'm sure. It'll be just the thing for Mr DeVere's crib,' she said, urging him to read some secret message into what she was saying. 'We'll have the star twinkling fit to bust, so to speak,' she enunciated pointedly. 'Now, off you go, Brabinger.'

Brabinger obliged and disappeared up the aisle, mystified at Audrey's change of heart.

DeVere was so pleased with himself for having produced this wonder of modern science, that he did not give Audrey's crib another thought – he now took it for granted that she, too, was now accepting his on its undoubted merits.

Indeed, she was peering into it with apparent awe and wonder, when there came a strident series of sounds as of short, sharp bleeps.

'What on earth's that funny noise?' enquired Marjory, looking at DeVere. He took his bleeper out of his pocket.

'It's all right. I'm wanted on the phone, that's all.'

Audrey still had her head in the crib.

'My goodness,' she said, 'there isn't a phone in here as well, is there?'

'How does the crib look?' asked old Mrs Polouvička as she was decorating the Christmas tree in the great hall that night.

'Very ritzy – I'd be pleased to live in it myself,' replied DeVere, irreverently.

Mrs Poo – as she had become known on the estate – stood back to admire her composition of tinsel and silver balls.

'Oh, my, we've come a long way, you and I, Bedrich.

You were too young to remember, but did I ever tell you about that Christmas you and I had all those years ago, just after your father died?'

'Often.'

'We were so poor, we just had a sprig of brushwood for a Christmas tree – and we couldn't afford decorations . . . .'

DeVere continued unpacking a crate of sherry and automatically mouthed her words with her.

'The two of us spent hours cutting up bits of orange peel, pictures from magazines and milk bottle tops – and for Christmas dinner we had carrot stew,' they recited in unison.

'But you know, in spite of all that,' went on the old lady on her own, 'looking back on it and thinking of all the Christmases that we've had before and since, that one was the most miserable of the lot.'

'What?' exclaimed DeVere, who had never heard that bit before.

'Mind you, at the time, if anyone had come to the door and offered us shop-bought stuff, we would have told them where to go.'

DeVere reflected for a moment. Was this not exactly what he had done to Audrey?

'Oh, my God, I've done it again,' he cried with self-reproach.

'What's wrong?' asked his mother.

'Audrey. What have I done to her?' he groaned.

'I dread to think, since she won't even come for Christmas Day.'

'Her crib. She couldn't come up with a crib, so she made one.'

'What out of?'

'Bits of orange peel and milk bottle tops, by the look of it.'

'How funny,' laughed the old lady. 'Just like our tree decorations.'

'Remember how we would have felt if anyone had trumped our decorations with something better?'

'We would have been hopping mad.'

'Just how Audrey is feeling now, I shouldn't wonder.'

He went to the door with some urgency.

'Where are you off to?' asked Mrs Poo.

'To the church. I'm going to withdraw my crib from the contest.'

By the time DeVere was back in the church, Brabinger had been getting busy fitting his homemade twinkling device to the guiding star, so Audrey, who was arranging some Christmas roses in the sanctuary, explained.

'As a matter of fact, he needn't have bothered,' said DeVere.

'What do you mean?' said Audrey.

'I mean, I've come to take my crib away. I think yours is much better.'

Audrey came down the chancel steps and faced him through an armful of laurel.

'How can you say that? There's clearly no comparison. I mean, we were so looking forward to seeing your heavenly bodies light up, and your guiding star twinkling.'

'But yours is better than mine,' he insisted.

'How can you say that?' she said, pointing at it down the side-aisle. 'You've got to admit it lacks a certain *je ne sais quoi*. That's French, by the way.'

'On the contrary, it has more *quoi* than mine,' said DeVere. Audrey was suspicious of what had brought about this change of heart.

'But we haven't seen yours in its full glory yet,' she said.

'Nor have I seen yours. Mine's going,' repeated DeVere, going to the table and trying to get a grip on the crib base.

'No, I insist. Mine is,' she said, going over to the side-aisle where hers was placed on a shelf above a radiator.

The rector, who came down the aisle at that moment,

sensed a quarrel was in progress, always a happy occurrence for him.

'Now, now, what's all this about?' he rebuked them.

'Oh, nothing, rector,' said DeVere innocently. 'It was just that we appear to have two cribs, and I think that we should have Mrs fforbes-Hamilton's.'

'And I insist that we have Mr DeVere's,' said Audrey.

'I see,' mused the rector. 'Then perhaps I should be the judge.'

They both agreed to this.

The rector looked at DeVere's crib with admiration.

'Oh, excellent, excellent,' he opined. But DeVere persisted. 'I think in view of the amount of work that has gone into Mrs fforbes-Hamilton's, hers is more in keeping with the spirit of Christmas.'

The rector turned round and looked at Audrey's effort. Above the radiator as it was, one of the figures had melted even more. Joseph was beginning to look decidedly drunk.

The rector's face crumpled at the spectacle, but he only let his amusement show fleetingly.

'Indeed,' he said, 'well, my impartial judgement is that I find myself taking Mrs fforbes-Hamilton's part in this dispute.'

The two contenders smiled a truce at each other.

'Yes, I quite agree with you,' continued the rector directing his remark to Audrey. 'We *should* have Mr DeVere's crib.'

He walked away, smiling. Audrey walked away, too. She was not smiling.

'Come along, Brabinger,' she fumed as she stormed through the vestry where the latter-day Edison was still at work with his wires, plugs and fuses.

'But, madam, I'm still trying to get this circuit right,' he said.

'Leave it,' she barked. 'Come along.'

On Christmas Eve the church looked beautiful with the sheen of evergreen shimmering with the flicker of a hundred candles. Come midnight, the church was packed with Medionites, and as the clock clunked the hour, Ned, the woodman, acting as verger, led the small procession of candle bearers and choir boys down the aisle to the refrain of 'Oh Come All Ye Faithful'.

Audrey and Marjory were in their customary places in the pew opposite DeVere and Mrs Polouvička. In fact, everybody was in their usual places, with the exception of Brabinger who, glad to be brought back to church, had slipped into the vestry to resume wiring-up the guiding star. One more connection and the job was done.

During the procession he peered out of the vestry door, waiting for a cue from the rector to throw the switch to illuminate the crib. At the end of the procession came the coped rector, and as he passed each pew, the congregation filed into the aisle and followed to the chancel steps where they gathered round the crib. They fanned out round the centrepiece and Audrey found herself pressed up against the wall by the vestry door.

'Happy Christmas, madam,' whispered Brabinger beaming through the door.

'What on earth are you doing in there, Brabinger?' she whispered back.

'I think I've managed to get Mr DeVere's star winking at last,' he said, proudly.

'You've done what?' exclaimed Audrey, tempering the volume of her voice in deference to her surroundings. 'I'd completely forgotten.'

'But you did say, madam, that I was to . . .'

It was too late for explanations. The hymn had faded away and all was silent, save for the tail end of their conversation which drew a stern look of reproach from DeVere and his mother.

'Let us pray,' intoned the vicar after a hiatus of coughing

and shuffling. 'Almighty God who, as on this night, did cause His only begotten Son to come down from heaven to be born, vouchsafe, we beseech Thee, so to bless and hallow this crib wherein are shown the wonders of that sacred birth. Amen.'

'Amen.'

Audrey held her breath in dread as the rector turned towards the vestry door and nodded to Brabinger.

Brabinger threw the switch. To Audrey's relief the lights in the crib came on without incident and the gibbous moon began to rise slowly into the night sky. The only technical problem was acoustic. The church organ had begun to play the introduction to 'O Little Town of Bethlehem' only to find itself competing with the tinny 'Jingle Bells' which issued from the back of the crib. But this tolerably manageable situation held good for only three seconds – the time factor in Brabinger's homemade circuit breaker.

On the fourth second, the lights in the crib and the guiding star went out again. But every other light in the church came on, blinding everybody in the congregation, whose eyes were accustomed to the near darkness which had prevailed hitherto. Simultaneously, the organ cut out and seemed to breathe its last, followed by three more seconds of stunned silence before it burst into life again.

Instantly, the church was once again plunged into darkness – whereupon the crib lights and the guiding star shone once more. Another three seconds of consternation elapsed before the organ was once more convulsed with its death rattle, and all attempts at a rendering of the hymn were abandoned.

The sudden switch in the direction of the current to power every light in the church, which now came on again, proved too much for the circuit. There was a loud explosion from behind the crib, the mechanism of which burst into flames and disintegrated in a cloud of smoke. No one could quite make out what had happened, for the church was once more in darkness and silence. The rumpus which followed was memorable in the annals of Grantleigh, notably for Brabinger's audible opinion of the switchboard which he expressed volubly as he laid into it with the full force of both fists and feet.

The Almighty had not vouchsafed to bless and hallow this crib.

The embarrassment of what became known as 'Brabinger's Bang' lived with Audrey throughout the following day. It cast a dark cloud over the whole of the Christmas proceedings, not that they had much going for them anyway.

Brabinger, needless to say, was in disgrace. His confinement to the kitchen was largely self-imposed.

Christmas lunch was a pretty gloomy affair for Audrey and Marjory, particularly as there wasn't much wine left after Brabinger had spent most of the morning drowning his sorrows. Pulling crackers and putting on the paper hats was done without enjoyment, and was no more than a gesture of acknowledgement that it was Christmas Day. In fact, the party was so miserable that even the cracker jokes seemed funny.

The only thing that cheered Audrey up was the Queen's Christmas broadcast. It consisted of spatchcocked footage of highlights of a royal tour. The bunting-festooned sports grounds and rows upon cheering rows of African children waving Union Jacks, enlivened within Audrey an hereditary shiver of pride in Britain's imperial past, in which her forbears had, by all accounts, played a glorious part.

'Isn't she sweet?' said Audrey when the Queen was done, as she turned the television off to avoid a circus. 'And to think she had to learn all that off by heart.'

During the broadcast, Marjory had been wondering what on earth could be done to liven up the day. Her conclusion was that a game of Charades might do the trick.

'Right,' she said, leaping out of the sofa. 'It's a book and a film.' She mimed the two media. 'Six words,' she went on, holding up seven fingers. With that, she grabbed a cushion from where she had been sitting and thrust it up the back of her cardigan and proceeded to hobble around the room pulling ugly faces and apparently heaving something long, thin and bendy down from the sky. Audrey watched the performance for a moment in amazement.

'Marjory, are you quite well?' she asked, absently cracking a Brazil nut.

'Well, apart from the hunch back . . .' she said in a gravel-toned French accent. 'Oh, I've given it away now.'

'Oh, so that's what you were doing. I thought you were punting down the Isis on a trampoline. What's it all about then?'

'Charades. It's time for party games now.'

'You can't play party games without a party,' objected Audrey as the Brazil nut shattered and shrapnelled the room.

'Come on, Aud,' enthused Marjory with false heartiness. 'At the manor we always used to have party games after Christmas dinner,' she added by way of persuasion.

'At the manor it was always Sardines,' Audrey sighed. 'That's the thing I'll miss most at Christmas.'

'We could play Sardines if you want to.'

'In a house this size? At the manor, squeezing oneself into a pokey hidey hole was a game – here it's a permanent state of affairs.'

'Well, we must do something. You won't even try. You've been a misery guts all day.'

'Of course I have. I don't deserve to be anything else after last night. I deliberately set out to ruin Richard's Christmas, and all I succeeded in doing is ruining mine and yours. I've made an absolute fool of myself.'

It had taken until now for Audrey to realize what she'd done, and what her motives had been. She had not simply forgotten to restrain Brabinger when she was fully aware in advance of the consequences of giving him his head. Hers had been a case of Freudian negligence. She had deliberately instigated and abetted the crib explosion. She intended to embarrass Richard DeVere to show him and the world that the Grantleigh estate could not function efficiently without her as its Queen Bee.

Meanwhile he had been amply proving that it could – nice, kind, conscientious, considerate, handsome, desirable Richard DeVere, whom she openly vilified and secretly idolized if she would but let herself, and whom she could not fault as a custodian of Grantleigh. Even if she could, and if she were going to be reinstalled there one day, he was the man she had to impress. And how was she going about it? Trying to elevate her own stature by constantly belittling his. The whole thing had backfired – it had literally blown up in her face.

'Everybody's enjoying themselves except you and me. We could have been over at the manor, too, if I hadn't been so stubborn and stupid. I bet they're having a wonderful time.'

Perhaps Audrey would have been consoled had she been able to see what was going on at the manor. Like herself and Marjory, DeVere and Mrs Polouvička were sitting gloomily in the drawing room by the fire, wearing token paper hats, surrounded by all the accoutrements of festivity – presents, decorations, food and drink – yet there was no sign of enjoyment.

Indeed, the old lady was most disgruntled at being deprived of Audrey's company, but refrained from extolling her virtues as a marriage prospect for her bachelor son. It only annoyed him.

'Oughtn't we to be *doing* something, mother,' said DeVere at the end of an intolerable silence, which made him think he was going deaf.

'It's getting dark,' said the old lady looking up from her knitting. 'Draw the curtains.'

DeVere got up from the chesterfield and walked to the big window, which spanned the length of the room. There, he cast a wistful glance at the lodge before drawing one of the curtains along its thick, brass rail. He returned to his seat – and resumed his bored posture.

'And what about the other one?' demanded his mother, seeing the window only half curtained.

'Not yet, mother,' said DeVere, languidly. 'We want to keep *something* to look forward to this evening.'

DeVere's wistful glance at the lodge betrayed that he was as mistaken in his assessment of Audrey's Christmas, as she had been about his. In spite of Audrey's instant refusal of his invitation, it never occurred to him that she wouldn't change her mind at the last moment.

After the events of the previous evening, she at least now owed him some kind of a favour. Had he not been doing his best to see that Christmas at Grantleigh was not conspicuously different from previous years? He had done it for her and Audrey had not appeared to appreciate this or give him credit.

Until this moment.

'The truth is that Richard has done everything in his power to see that everybody on the estate has a good Christmas, including us, and I've thrown everything back in his face,' Audrey was saying, almost choking with shame and humility.

'Don't be so hard on yourself.'

'If I hadn't been so pig-headed, we could have been over there with them now, playing Sardines.'

'Yes, it used to be very intimate when we were all packed away in a hidey hole, didn't it?' Marjory remembered.

'I remember I once hid in an old butler's silver safe one year and Marton was the first to find me. It quite revived our marriage – until I realized who it was.'

'You should have gone to the manor, you really should.'

'Yes, I know I should,' Audrey admitted.

'Still, if you didn't want to . . .'

Audrey snapped at her.

'Of course I wanted to. For obvious reasons. But no, I had to insist on spending my first Christmas alone, just to prove that I'm not the sort of person who cracks up easily. Well, it's not true. It's all a sham.' She allowed a single sob to escape, and might have given way to her emotions, were it not for the fairy lights on the Christmas tree which suddenly and unaccountably lit up.

The two of them looked at the tree, amazed. Three seconds later, the lights went off again.

'Brabinger was right,' laughed Audrey, suddenly brightening. 'They do flash on and off – every two days!'

But they came on again and winked merrily at three second intervals – there had been a circuit breaker attachment on it all the time.

They laughed and the heart-rending atmosphere of the previous few minutes vanished as Audrey became her old self again. They laughed so long and loud that they did not hear the door bell.

The door opened and Brabinger came in a little the worse for drink. He blew a fanfare on a plastic kazoo, courtesy of the Fabfun Novelty Company, who made the crackers.

'Brabinger, what are you up to?'

'Sounding a fanfare, madam. Heralding your visitors.'

'Visitors?'

'Mr DeVere and his mother, madam.'

The two women leapt up and raced to get to the wall-mirror first, where they attended to their own appearance, apparently using the other's reflection. They hardly had time for more than a wiped eye and a hair pat each, before DeVere and Mrs Polouvička were in the room.

They bore gifts – bottles of champagne and boxes of chocolates and crystallized fruits. The exchange of greeting left no-one in any doubt that everybody was very pleased to see each other and that as far as the spirit of Christmas was concerned, this moment was to be a turning point.

'What brings you here?' asked Audrey, trying to contain her excitement.

'We were bored,' said the old lady, with disarming honesty.

'We thought we'd join your party,' agreed DeVere. 'You look as though you're having a wonderful time.'

'Oh, yes, we are, aren't we, Marjory?'

'Are we?' said Marjory, wide-eyed. 'Well, we are now I suppose, yes.'

Brabinger coughed.

'Drinks anybody?' he asked.

'Oh, thank you,' said DeVere.

Brabinger coughed again, and stood in silence eyeing the bottles in DeVere's arms, before DeVere took the hint and handed them over.

'This is going to be fun,' said Audrey, smiling radiantly. 'You've joined us just in time for Sardines.'

'Oh, no,' said Mrs Poo, collapsing into the sofa. 'I couldn't eat another thing.'

'It's a game,' explained Marjory.

'Sounds fun,' said DeVere.

Audrey was anxious to get everybody organized at once.

'Right. I'll be it. And I bet you never find me.'

She made for the door, and as she passed DeVere she whispered in his ear.

'I'll be in the broom cupboard under the stairs.'

'What do we do?' protested DeVere. 'I've never played this game before.'

Audrey turned in the doorway.

'Splendid,' she said, 'then I'll have to teach you. Come with me.'

She took his hand and led him out of the room. The two unattached women left in the room looked at each other with amazement – Marjory at Audrey's sudden lift of spirits, and Mrs Polouvička speculating what her son and Audrey might be getting up to – with any luck.

The door opened again and Audrey looked in fleetingly.

'Now, hide your eyes, you two, and start counting,' she said gleefully. 'To a million.'

She disappeared into the hall again hooting with laughter.

2

Let discretion draw a veil over what took place between Audrey and DeVere in the broom cupboard in the space of the ten seconds it took Marjory to count to a million and find them there. It couldn't have been consummate, but it must have been promising, for their relationship took an instant upturn which began the longest spree of good feeling they had ever had – all of two days.

During the truce, Audrey began to see DeVere in a different light and to regard him in the long term, conceding that he was now almost a suitable match for her – almost, but there was no hurry.

For his part, DeVere began to think more seriously about that thing which Audrey cared about most profoundly – the Grantleigh estate. Then suddenly he announced his intention to take over its farming personally – and that was his second big mistake.

It was almost New Year and DeVere had set himself a target to put the Grantleigh estate in profit by the end of the following year. He'd already paved the way for his dramatic declaration by having feasibility studies undertaken, taking expert advice from the Cavendish Foods Agricultural Production department, and installing a computer in the farm office – he wasn't the man to make extravagant public claims without being pretty certain that he could deliver. But he was not being entirely altruistic – doing it just for Audrey. His plan was to make Grantleigh a fully accredited supplier of some single crop to Cavendish Foods, but to have the estate tender competitively with the rest.

In short, DeVere had been having new ideas – phenomena to which the Grantleigh estate had, over the years, developed total resistance. Nobody was more immune to change – even its most virulent strains – than Audrey.

She had been thinking only the day before whilst out for her afternoon constitutional with Bertie, how wonderful the estate was looking, with its mosaic of fields, hedgerows and woodlands, its hills and dells, its lakes and streams. And she thanked providence that whilst all else in the country was changing out of all recognition, at least Grantleigh looked the same.

But she did not permit providence to take full credit. That would leave the endeavours of the local Countryside Conservancy Association unsung, and this conscientious little body had, over the years, successfully baulked at suggestions of through roads, housing estates, pylons and nuclear power stations, and had managed to nip most threats of development in the bud.

Although Richard DeVere had done nothing to despoil the countryside, its committee – on which Audrey served as what was known as a rotating member – could not help feeling apprehensive that the plans for Grantleigh, of which he spoke when he first saw the place and which had been lying dormant, might suddenly burst into life again.

It was inevitably one of the topics of conversation in the manor rooms four days before the end of the year at the annual meeting of the Conservancy Association. It was quite an exciting occasion by Grantleigh standards, since the speaker was none other than Sir Peter Allenshaw, the association's pioneer and leading light.

'You people are the backbone of the movement,' explained Sir Peter over coffee after his talk, 'Life in the Hedgerows'. He was being feted by Brigadier Lemington, the chairman, Marjory and Audrey – the ruling triumvirate of the branch.

'You are our watchdogs in the field, and that is where the abuse of the environment is happening,' Sir Peter went on.

'I can assure you that there have been no abuses of the environment here,' Audrey said proudly, mindful of her recent impression of the estate's unspoilt beauty.

'So far, but you never know with these city farmers like Mr DeVere,' said Sir Peter, emphatically.

The mention of DeVere drew attention to his absence. Audrey made a mental note to enquire into his excuses for it, and changed the subject.

'How is your wife, Sir Peter?'

'Oh, I didn't know you knew her.'

'Well, we once stood next to each other at Ascot. But not for long. Our dresses clashed.'

'So you wouldn't have known her well enough to know that she died last year?'

Audrey blushed and swallowed hard.

'I'm so sorry. I didn't realize,' she stammered shamefully.

A silence fell upon the group. All one could hear was the distant conversation between Ned and the rector on the other side of the room.

'Very good talk,' the rector was saying, 'but I think Sir Peter was wrong to talk about a *flock* of duck. It's a flock of sheep – like it's a gaggle of geese, but I'm not sure what it is of duck. Do you know, Ned?'

'A casserole, I believe,' suggested Ned. He wasn't really listening, but was trying to help himself to a sandwich from a plate carried by Mrs Beacham, the cook and dogsbody at the manor, who was making a beeline for the group of officers and their guests. She slapped his wrist so that he dropped it back on the plate.

'Sandwiches anyone?' offered Mrs Beacham.

The brigadier hovered over them eagerly.

'What are they?' said Sir Peter as he raised his hand to help himself.

'Pheasant pâté – homemade.'

Sir Peter's hand and his face fell.

'Oh,' he said, 'I'd rather not. I'm a vegetarian'.

This dared the others to declare their own dietary preferences, which were not those of dedicated conservationists.

They all fell back and let Mrs Beacham continue her round.

'No, the problem is that the whale and the white rhino seem to get all the publicity,' Sir Peter went on, as if this statement were connected with either his dead wife or the sandwich. 'You don't get much support for saving mere hedgerows.'

'Well, we don't get many white rhino on this estate,' said Audrey, breezily, trying to redeem her social gaffe which now seemed forgotten.

The conversation continued until Mrs Beacham returned with another plate of sandwiches. The brigadier took one, and bit into it, while the group glared disapprovingly at him.

'It's cheese and cucumber,' he explained innocently. That made it all right for the others to help themselves.

'What did you think it was?' laughed the brigadier. 'White rhino?'

The following morning, Audrey determined to seek out Richard DeVere and pass on the benefit of Sir Peter's plea on behalf of the beleaguered hedgerows. She could not have known how timely such a lecture would have been, for the hedges were the subject consuming farmer DeVere's attention that very morning.

He was in the farm office with his jacket off and sleeves rolled up, poring over maps of the estate with Miller, the farm foreman.

'We're losing acres of good productive land here,' he was insisting, as if trying to drum a very simple idea into an even simpler head.

They were looking at a patchwork of fields and hedgerows round Thornberry Woods on the northern side of the valley.

'There must be twenty little fields there. It looks like a slice of salami. Why?'

'Always been like that, sir.'

'But why can't we have just one, say, fifty-acre field, and then we can have one single crop.'

'You can't have just one field. Not with all them hedges.'

'Exactly. So let's get rid of them. They're a waste of good land.'

'But if I may say so, Mr DeVere . . .'

Whether he may have said so or not was immaterial once Audrey was in the room.

'Have you been giving Mr DeVere the benefit of your advice, Mr Miller?' she asked as she threw open the door.

'I was trying, Mrs fforbes-Hamilton, but . . .'

'That will be all, Miller. Look into it, would you?' ordered DeVere, dismissing him with a gesture.

'If you say so,' grumbled the foreman as he left the office, muttering 'city farmers' as he shuffled out.

Audrey sat down in the chair opposite DeVere's desk as if she intended to stay.

'Do you have an appointment?' mocked DeVere with the kind of levity their relationship now permitted.

Audrey looked at her watch.

'Yes, I do. And if this takes too long, I'll be late for it,' she said. 'I'm late as it is because I've been looking all over the place for you. I didn't expect to find you in the farm office.'

'Isn't that where you'd expect to find a busy farmer?'

'A busy farmer, yes – but not you.'

DeVere got up to gain the advantage of height so that the

forthcoming dressing down would go in the right direction.

'Yes, I happen to be a busy farmer, and I'm getting on with the job of putting this place back on its feet after years of mismanagement.'

He played straight into Audrey's hands.

'Then why weren't you at the Countryside Conservancy meeting last night? You would have learnt a lot. Sir Peter Allenshaw's talk might have been entirely for your benefit.'

Neither of them could have appreciated the accuracy of this sally.

'I'm sure it was,' said DeVere, 'but I've got too many people around here trying to tell me how to run this estate. All you get are cockeyed ideas which are years out of date and don't make good business sense.'

Audrey stiffened.

'Grantleigh is a way of life. It's not supposed to be a business.'

'Then it should be. Only an incompetent idiot would fail to make a profit out of an estate this size.'

'We never did.'

DeVere gestured to show that this was just his point, but soon despaired of ever making Audrey see that a failure to make a profit was anything but a matter of pride. He felt that if the flaws in her thinking were to be rectified at all, it would be by the tactic of patient, paternal explanation, which he didn't have time for at this moment. Suffice it to say –

'In a few days time, Audrey, it will be New Year's Day. Now, if I haven't made a profit by this time next year, I shall pack up and go back to London.'

'Oh, dear,' sniffed Audrey, 'we shall all miss you dreadfully.'

If DeVere's New Year's resolution was ambitious and praiseworthy, Audrey's, if it could be called a resolution at all, was neither. She resolved simply never to be caught out again with a social gaffe on the scale she committed in the matter of Lady Allenshaw's demise.

To substantiate her resolution, Audrey invested in some back numbers of *The Times* – to study the hatch-match-and-despatch columns and keep tabs on the society news which she had lately been neglecting, with the humiliating consequences of the Conservancy meeting *faux pas*. She managed to arrange a stay of execution for old newspapers collected for recycling by the local St John's Ambulance Brigade.

For the period of her research and note-taking, Audrey's entire conversation consisted of news of the nobility and landed gentry and titled people. It consumed her to such an extent that she even neglected her regular afternoon walk with Bertie. It led Marjory to the conclusion that she was taking the matter too far.

'Are you coming for a walk?' Marjory asked one afternoon.

'No, I'm getting all the exercise I need, thank you.'

'Yes. Just walking between the sofa and the bookcase and heaving *Who's Who and Debrett's* in and out of the shelves all day. Maybe it is all right for you, but not for Bertie.'

Audrey put down her notes and papers, and allowed herself to be persuaded out of the house for Bertie's sake.

Soon the two friends and the dog could be seen wandering along the north side of the valley where the brook ran along the edge of Thornberry Woods.

'I think you're taking all this titles business too far,' said Marjory, having plucked up courage to broach the subject.

'I'm just doing my homework, that's all.'

'At that meeting, you were all over Sir Peter Allenshaw. It wasn't anything to do with his talk on hedgerows – you just couldn't get it out of your mind that he was *Sir* Peter.'

'Don't keep saying *Sir* Peter like that – you sound like an American.'

'You're not really interested in countryside conservancy

at all, are you?' challenged Marjory at last.

Audrey stopped and rounded on her, her eyes blazing.

'I don't know how you can say such a thing, Marjory. There's not a hedgerow or a thicket on this estate that I don't love. Look over there.'

She pointed towards the edge of the woods where an old elm tree stood.

'Well, every bird and squirrel that has ever visited that tree, I happen to know personally. Even when I came here as a child, I used to love that tree. We used to climb it – we had a swing on it. That's how you come to know about nature. You grow up with it.'

Audrey's singling out an isolated tree as a symbol of her abiding love for nature in general focused Marjory's attention on the tree. It made her aware of a sensation which for the last few moments had been gnawing away at her subconscious – the distant hum of a chainsaw – a sound alternating between a whine and a groan as it made contact with wood. The sound was competing with Audrey's raised voice.

'So don't tell me I don't care about nature as if I were some kind of town planner, because if any part of this estate is so much as touched, you know that I'd be the first person to leap to its protection.'

The sound of the chainsaw was coming from the direction in which Audrey pointed. It was confirmed by a sudden tilt in the angle of the tree – then it twisted slightly before sweeping through its arc to the ground, with a creak and a crash of broken branches which they seemed to be hearing long after the tree had disappeared from view.

'Oh, my lord,' shrieked Audrey, galvanized into action.

The two women ran for all they were worth to the edge of the field and peered over the hedge to where the tree had been. There they saw old Ned well pleased with himself, counting the rings on the exposed tree stump.

'One hundred and fifty years old, give or take. Shame

eh?' said the old man. To Audrey, this was the understatement of the year.

'Ned, what do you mean by cutting this down?'

'Orders of Mr DeVere, Mrs fforbes-Hamilton. We're clearing this bit of land so that we can get at the hedgerows.'

What sacrilege was this?

'The hedgerows, Ned?' asked Marjory in amazement.

'Yes. This one here and all the ones up to the top of the hill – so this'll be all one field.'

'Whatever for?' said Audrey.

'Dunno, ma'am.'

'Is this Mr DeVere's doing?'

'Yes, and I'll be glad to see the back of these hedges,' said Ned. 'If you have to drive a tractor in this lot, always going round corners, always turning in the headlands . . .'

Audrey did not see it quite this way.

'Ned, you are paid to go round corners.'

Audrey was so shocked by Ned's revelation that she stood speechless for a moment while she thought what could be done.

'Marjory, we must mobilize.'

'We certainly must. I've heard of city farmers trying to turn England into the prairies, but I never thought it would happen here.'

'If he's digging up these hedges, then he'll have to dig me up with them – and you, Marjory.'

When an idea engages the spirit of the English upper classes, its emotional aspects at once give way to practical considerations. Within seconds, strategy was riding on anger's chariot.

'Now, you go and tell the brigadier, and we'll hold an emergency meeting of the Conservancy Association in the lodge immediately. Then we'll organize a demonstration – and ring the local paper to send a photographer.'

Audrey rattled off a great list of things to be done by way of launching what, in a few seconds, already became a fully fledged campaign to save hedgerows. Marjory strained her brain to remember them all.

'And meanwhile, I'm going to go straight over to see Mr DeVere and read him the riot act,' Audrey announced defiantly, and started to walk towards the manor.

Ned stood on the tree stump the other side of the hedge and looked across to the two women.

'So what am I supposed to be doing?' he asked.

Audrey looked back at him.

'Well, for a start, you can put that tree back up again,' she said.

DeVere was a difficult character for the Grantleigh old guard to fathom. Among the most perplexed was Miller, the farm foreman, who, even though he knew DeVere was wrong, credited him with some nous, and indeed the Midas touch which had placed him at the head of his grocery empire. He could not bring himself to challenge him.

'If you say so, sir,' was about the extent of his conversation with DeVere. And now he had acquiesced against his better judgement in the matter of the desecration of hedgerows.

'Just get the machinery in, and get on with it,' was the last of DeVere's orders he felt duty bound to obey.

Added to DeVere's own record of success was the say-so of his newly installed computer in which he had been placing what, to Miller, seemed a disproportionate amount of faith and confidence. Any solution which printed itself out on the computer console was at once insisted upon. If DeVere, backed by the computer, said 'Dig up the hedgerows on the northern slopes of Grantleigh', it must be the right thing to do.

Miller had just finished telephoning the hire company to arrange for the JCB earth movers to come in and see to the job, when Audrey barnstormed the farm office.

'What in heaven's name are you doing tearing the estate

apart?' she demanded, not waiting for an invitation to speak.

'What are you talking about?' asked DeVere, not looking up from the computer.

'The hedgerows.'

'Oh, the hedgerows. So you've heard about them?'

'It's true, is it? Have you no respect for the countryside?'

'Yes, but I've also got a healthy respect for my bank balance,' he said, continuing to press the keys of the computer, from which buzzes and whistles issued.

He drew Audrey's attention to the computer. It was the first Audrey had seen of it, and she peered over the top so that she saw the keyboard.

'And what's this?' she demanded to know. 'A Junior Printing Kit?'

'A computer. This machine can do in a few seconds everything that your family has achieved in centuries.'

'I see,' said Audrey coolly. 'So it fights crusades, does it? You can programme it to rule India?'

'No, in this instance, it's merely suggesting we convert twenty impractical little fields into one practical fifty-acre field.'

'I thought as much,' Audrey sighed. 'Very well, Richard. I think it is only fair to tell you that your abuse of our environment will be resisted by every means at our disposal.'

DeVere was not intimidated.

'Do what you think is necessary,' he said. 'But I hope that won't stand in the way of your organizing the New Year's Eve party on the estate.'

The New Year's Eve party was something Audrey had completely forgotten about. While she welcomed the indication that DeVere had not forgotten about it, and that this Grantleigh tradition was being observed, she found his timing of the request that she should organize it, the ultimate impudence.

'Certainly it will,' she said angrily. 'I don't know how you could ask such a thing in the circumstances.' She made for the door.

'Well, don't let me stand in the way of the great white heat of British technology,' she said sarcastically, glancing at the back of the computer which, with its bleeps and its buzzes, seemed to be engaging DeVere's entire attention. She swept out of the room.

DeVere hardly noticed that she had gone. Such was his dismay at the figures on the computer screen, which indicated that he had lost yet another game of electronic table tennis.

Soon the Grantleigh 'Save Our Hedgerows' campaign was coming along well. Marjory had been busy on the phone, rallying support, and before long the brigadier was round at the lodge, organizing the strategy like a military operation.

'Can't have him chopping things down like that,' he said, adding the military argument for good measure. 'Can't run an army without bushy-topped trees – wouldn't know what to fire at.'

He spread out a map of the estate on the table and began to bark orders as if he were haranguing a battalion rather than talking to two women in a small room.

'That's the area we have to protect. All these fields north of Thornberry Woods. The only way for a vehicle is down Long Lane or the Marlbury Road on the north. So we post pickets here – and here,' he ordered, jabbing the map with a wrinkled forefinger. 'And I'll have my command post here.'

'That's the Mortlake Arms.'

'Is it?' said the brigadier in amazement. 'So it is,' he conceded, as if he didn't know.

Having composed the wording of the placards which the demonstrators were going to carry, the question of who the demonstrators would be, where they would come from, how many of them there were likely to be, and where the pickets would be deployed, had to be tackled.

'I've arranged a coach to collect about forty members of the Conservancy Association from other areas, who have promised to help,' said Audrey, who had been on the phone for the previous half hour.

'Have them report to me at the pub – er – command post,' said the brigadier.

For the next two days, Audrey found the whole idea of this campaign of consummate interest. It was just up her street, and, like anything that suited her, she devoted herself to it wholeheartedly – at least until something better came up.

Miller, the foreman, proved a useful ally, and he kept her posted on developments – it was he who informed her that JCB earth movers were moving in on New Year's Eve. She immediately reported this intelligence to the brigadier.

'JCB? What's that?' said the brigadier.

'It's an earth mover.'

'Sounds more like something out of the New Year's Honours List.'

If anything was likely to distract Audrey from the job, it was mention of the Honours List – the subject of titles and heredity having been her most recent crusade. That the JCB should put her in mind of the Honours List made sense, but why the brigadier? She asked him.

'Oh, it was just, well, nothing really. Just a whisper, you know,' he faltered defensively.

Anything that was just a whisper was of great fascination to Audrey.

'Do you know something, brigadier?' she asked.

'No, no. Shouldn't have mentioned it.'

'You *do* know something, don't you?'

'Only that I gather that the New Year's Honours List is worth keeping an eye on this year.'

'Something that might interest us? Or somebody?'

'Oh, somebody, certainly.'

'Not Richard DeVere?'

'No, no,' he hedged. 'I promised not to let on.'

'It is DeVere, isn't it?'

'Sorry, Audrey, not another word. Shouldn't have said anything at all.'

'I think you've said enough for me to guess, brigadier.'

'Then for Lord's sake, keep it to yourself. We don't want any trouble.'

At once the information was passed on to Marjory.

'I wonder what he'll get?' she said.

'Probably a Kindly Call Me God.'

'A what?'

'KCMG. Or possibly a Royal Warrant by appointment to Her Majesty the Queen – Grocer.'

'You don't think they'll make him a life peer?' suggested Marjory enthusiastically.

'Lord DeVere – gosh.'

It was not until dinner that evening that the full implications of DeVere's possible inclusion in the New Year's Honours List dawned upon Audrey.

Brabinger had served stewed plums which had left her with an aftermath of stones on the side of the plate. There were four of them.

'Tinker, tailor, soldier, sailor,' she mused, flicking them into the middle of the plate, and then bringing them out on to the rim again.

'Coach, carriage, wheelbarrow, dustcart. Silk, satin, cotton, rags.'

The signs were not encouraging when it came to the question of whom she would marry and in what – so far, a sailor, in rags, riding in a dustcart. Counting plumstones in this way was traditional family routine, which she continued to equate with her future marriage prospects, even long after she was married to Marton. Now she was single again, she had revived it with great interest.

'Would you like one more plum?' said Brabinger knowingly, having observed what was going on.

'Yes, please,' she said. She disposed of the food rapidly, and eagerly added the stone to the rim of her plate.

'Tinker, tailor, soldier, sailor – rich man,' she exulted. 'Silk, satin, cotton, rags – silk. Coach, carriage, wheelbarrow, dustcart – coach.'

She searched the mind for other sequences, and one came to her from her childhood, which she had not used for years.

'Soldier brave, soldier blue, dashing airman, oxford blue. *Squire so hale*.'

Five plum stones. Six would have had her 'taking the veil'. But this new configuration, espoused her to a squire so hale. Now she was getting somewhere.

'This year, next year, sometime, never. *This year*.'

There was enough favourable evidence in the portents to make her take it seriously. It was only when Brabinger pointed out that there were only three days left of this year that she realized she had been speaking her thoughts aloud.

Audrey tried to change the subject – but it was only after she switched the conversation to the news that Richard DeVere might be mentioned in the New Year's Honours List, that she realized that she hadn't changed the subject at all.

'Oh, how interesting, milady,' said Brabinger.

She looked up, startled.

'Brabinger, you called me milady. Why?'

'Oh, did I, madam?' he said. 'How curious. Perhaps I was just thinking of Sir Richard DeVere – Sir Richard and Lady DeVere, madam.'

'Brabinger, there is no Lady DeVere.'

'I know, madam. That means there's a vacancy.'

The thought of the vacant situation caused Audrey to think wistfully about her relationship with Richard DeVere.

'It is *Mr* DeVere – at least for the next three days.'

At present the situation was one of war between them – at least until the matter of the hedgerows was settled. Yet now it suddenly became a matter of urgency to ingratiate herself with him before he was entitled or ennobled – lest her sudden interest in him be interpreted as arrant social climbing.

'Amends must be made at once,' she thought, casting all her commitments to the hedgerows campaign to the wind, and going to the phone to ring the manor. The voice on the other end of the phone sounded already dignified and noble – in contrast to her own which stuttered and blurted apologies for her tirade the previous day.

'I disapprove strongly of your actions, of course, but it was quite wrong of me to come and tell you so.'

He accepted the apology in the spirit in which it was tendered.

'And by way of making up for it, I'd be delighted to accept your invitation to act as hostess at the New Year's Eve party.'

The telephone conversation left DeVere mystified as to what had caused this complete capitulation and *volte face*.

A letter to the same effect as that phone call might have ended 'your obedient servant'. That was certainly the role Audrey was fulfilling by New Year's Eve, and – odd for her – contentedly. That afternoon she was to be found throwing her weight about in the manor room, organizing the New Year's party in DeVere's name. The fact that she had another appointment – demonstrating down at Thornberry Woods with Marjory and the brigadier and a flying squad of conservationists – was nowhere in her thoughts.

But her absence from the picket line did not go unnoticed – in fact, it so enraged Marjory that after several hours of blockading the threatened hedgerows, she was calling Audrey all sorts of names one would not have thought were even in her vocabulary. By mid-afternoon, without the excitement which the appearance of earth movers might have aroused, one would have thought, to hear Marjory, that Audrey was the villain of the whole piece, and that the mud pies which the demonstrators had made to hurl at the JCBs were intended for her.

By late afternoon, cold, tired and hungry, Marjory had almost forgotten what she was demonstrating about. In fact, when DeVere himself appeared on the picket line to enquire what all the disturbance was about, she was actually quite shocked when a few pickets pelted his Range-Rover with mud pies and forced him to make himself scarce.

Before DeVere had had a chance to recognize any of his assailants, his hasty retreat took him to the manor room, which he entered in a state of conspicuous agitation, his face showing signs of shock, bewilderment and mud.

'That is absolutely disgraceful,' Audrey reacted sympathetically when he told her what had happened. 'It was supposed to be a peaceful demonstration.'

'So you know something about it, do you?'

'It's just Marjory and her countryside conservationist cronies. I decided to have nothing to do with it.'

'To do with what?'

'Picketing Thornberry Woods to stop you tearing up the hedgerows.'

DeVere searched his memory and laughed.

'Oh, that. I'd forgotten all about that.'

'After all, they are your hedgerows. You are entitled to do what you like with them.'

'But I'm not going to do anything with them.'

'You're not?'

'No. I scrapped that idea. I took expert advice and decided it was a bad idea.'

'Really?'

'Yes, that's a north-facing slope over there – if I'd grubbed up the hedges, it would expose the whole area to storm damage – I'm not going to save a few acres at the risk of losing the whole crop, now am I?'

With that, he went off to clean himself up, leaving Audrey with an item of invaluable information with which, handled skilfully, she could resolve her whole dilemma.

Hell hath no fury like a woman left standing out in the cold all day. When Ned, who happened to be passing the picket line, disclosed Audrey's whereabouts, Marjory spun round on her heels and cut across the fields in the direction of the manor rooms, followed by the brigadier who could hardly keep up.

'Don't tread mud into the carpet,' screamed Audrey as they threw open the door of the newly decorated manor room, before they had a chance to spend their fury.

'So this is where you've been skulking, is it?' accused Marjory.

'Desertion, that's what it is – court martial offence,' thundered the brigadier in support. 'Where were you?'

Audrey remained infuriatingly calm, self-possessed and unrattled. She knew what was coming, and had steeled herself for it. She intended to capitalize on it.

'I was attending to my duties here,' she said coolly.

'Your duty was out there picketing the hedgerows.'

'Yes, but we frightened them off, didn't we? No sign of the enemy all day,' added the brigadier.

'I know,' said Audrey smugly. Her accusers fell silent for a moment.

'You know?' said Marjory. 'What do you know?'

'The whole operation's been cancelled.'

'You knew that and didn't tell us?' screamed Marjory.

'No need to blow your top, Marjory. You should be pleased. Your hedges and your wildlife are safe.'

'Oh, I am pleased, but what's been happening?'

Audrey preened herself.

'I always said that reasoned diplomacy was much more

effective than your kind of Bolshevism,' she lectured. 'And thanks to me, Mr DeVere has abandoned his plans for the Thornberry Wood hedgerows.'

The two conservationists breathed a sigh of relief.

'How the blazes did you manage that?' asked the brigadier.

'I simply told him that if he destroyed the hedgerows, he'd expose his crop to storm damage, by losing all that he would gain by taking the hedgerows away.'

'So we've won?'

'Yes, and no thanks to slinging mud at people's cars,' sneered Audrey pointedly. 'Now, I think you'd better clean yourselves up and get changed for the party tonight,' she added sweetly.

Marjory and the brigadier had forgotten all about the party. They had both refused DeVere's invitation.

'Seemed like fraternization with the enemy,' explained the brigadier.

'Well, he's not the enemy now, is he? The war's over,' said Audrey. 'Anyway, I'm the hostess now, and I'm inviting you.'

It turned out to be quite a party. It started quietly, but soon took on the full festive spirit which Audrey did much to enhance by leading the conga over the rector's bicycle. However, she was just killing time until she could tackle DeVere with the subject foremost in her mind – the contents of the Honours List. Midnight struck – and the New Year formalities were observed, whereupon Audrey broke abruptly out from the *Auld Lang Syne* circle and buttonholed DeVere.

'Well, Happy New Year, Richard,' she said, and without waiting for a reply, blurted, 'It's the first of January. Isn't there something you want to tell me?'

'I don't know. Is there?' said DeVere, mystified.

'Don't keep us in suspense any longer. It'll be published

in a few hours.'

'What will?'

'The New Year's Honours List, of course. And *somebody* is rumoured to be in it.' She nudged him, knowingly.

DeVere looked bewildered and stared at her blankly. A stalling device, Audrey suspected.

'Oh, yes, I did hear something,' he said at last.

'Tell me.'

'No, no, it's not for me to say.'

Audrey was not at first distracted by a whoop of delight and an outbreak of applause from the group behind her. But when Marjory and the brigadier detached themselves from it and hurtled in her direction, nearly bowling her over, she could not ignore it.

'Marjory, what on earth's going on?' she asked.

'Guess what?' gushed Marjory. 'The brigadier has just told me.'

'Told you what?'

'He's getting a CBE for services to conservation.'

Well, if this wouldn't draw DeVere out, nothing would, Audrey thought.

'A CBE? Huh,' she sniffed, 'wait till you hear what Mr DeVere has to tell us.' She looked at him expectantly. 'Well, Richard, what were you going to tell me?'

'Just that,' he said. 'Brigadier Lemington is getting a CBE for services to conservation. Swore me to secrecy, of course, but if he's telling you . . .'

The brigadier interjected.

'Shouldn't have said anything really. Bad form.'

Audrey arched.

'You mean you're not getting anything?' said Audrey, listing in her mind the compromises she had made on the strength of at least a knighthood.

'Lord, no,' said DeVere, and roared with laughter.

'So, it was the brigadier,' huffed Audrey to herself, thinking better of letting rip her anger at being deceived, when she realized that she was the only party to any deception. She had deceived herself.

DeVere was talking to her, but she could hardly hear.

'You know, Audrey, you should keep in with him – Brigadier Lemington, CBE. Bit of a title, eh? He could be a useful chap to know socially. Next stop a knighthood. . . .'

But Audrey was already on her way home.

3

Audrey was perfectly aware that her anger with Richard DeVere was quite unjustified, yet she could not suppress it. While it lasted, she was on the look out for some other misdemeanour or pecadillo on his past which might give her reasonable cause to feel the way she did about him. She had only to wait until the following Saturday.

With the week's work done, Saturday on the estate was the most popular day of the week – unless, of course, you were a pheasant. Throughout autumn and winter – the shooting season – the pheasant has only to take to the air on a Saturday, and the chances of it encountering a spray of lead pellets hurtling towards it at high speed are great. Those that stay aground have only to be minding their own business in a patch of kale to find themselves being harassed by a pack of dogs and men beating their way through the undergrowth with large sticks and yelling at the tops of their voices when a pheasant takes wing. Saturdays at Grantleigh, there is nothing for pheasants to do except hope for darkness to fall before they do. It's a curious fact that in all the years that man and pheasants have lived together neither has evolved a better method of shooting or avoiding being shot. It takes nine men with guns and twenty beaters, all with dogs and full complement of vehicles, a whole day on average to bag seventy brace – a poor return on a large investment. Furthermore, the economics are rather shaky; they say ten pounds goes up and one pound comes down.

And as for the pheasant, one would have thought that there was something in its inherited instincts which would lead it to seek out some inaccessible place to lie low on Saturdays from October to January. But no.

It is a measure of DeVere's preoccupation with his own business affairs and new-found farming interests, that a gang of hearties could burst into the great hall every Saturday morning, filling the manor with ya-hooing and cigar smoke, to prime their weapons and then file out into the winter morning and poop off all over the estate, without him being aware of it. It was well into the season before he even noticed the shoot. When he at last awoke to its existence he thought he ought to take up the sport himself. He therefore wrote 'shoot myself' on his list of 'Things to Do', an item which caused him considerable perplexity when it came to the top of the pile that Saturday.

Knowing shooting to be part of the lifestyle of the English gentleman, he embraced the sport wholeheartedly. Taking counsel from Sir Grafton Willoughby, his counterpart on the neighbouring Moneymore Park, on the social and sartorial aspects of the sport, and from Hawkins, the gamekeeper, on its practical elements and statistics, he was soon fully equipped and ready to take the field.

It was an exceptionally chilly morning that he appeared to have chosen for his first foray into the sport. At least it seemed so when he got up, dressed in his new shooting clothes and went downstairs to the gun room to get his new Purdeys out of their case. He took them through to the drawing room where he preened himself in the long mirror, striking aggressive poses with one of the guns. Yes, he certainly looked the part – a combination of primordial hunter and perfect English gentleman. The Norfolk jacket, the felt hat, the check shirt, the plus-fours, and of course, the moustache – yes, that helped, too, even though he had had it for over twenty years.

His moment of self-esteem was interrupted by his mother

who came into the room carrying one of his old jumpers.

'What do you call that?' she said, holding out one of the sleeves.

'A hole,' said DeVere.

'How can a son of mine get his clothes in such a state?'

'It's a gift.'

'No wonder Audrey will not look at you,' said the old lady, offering a new variation on an old theme. She scrutinized her son, taking in the new outfit.

'What are you dressed like that for?' she demanded. 'You look like a string bean.'

'I'm shooting today.'

'Shooting? But it must be freezing out there. Are you wearing your woolly vest?'

'Three – and I'll be carrying a spare.'

Mrs Polouvička found the prospect of venturing into the open an act of lunacy.

'Fancy going out there with nothing on.'

'I haven't got nothing on.'

'You'll catch your death. Still, as they say in old Czechoslovakia, "A naked man fears no pickpockets". You English – you're as mad as hatters.'

An Englishman would have regarded this as a compliment, but if there was one thing guaranteed to anger DeVere, it was a cynical aspersion about his nationality. After all, being English was his main crusade in life, and he had still to master the finer points of the pose of an English gentleman. He had yet to learn that a touch of madness was Englishness in its ultimate form. He took his mother's remark seriously, and turned on her angrily.

'So, mad are we? Well, before you start coming on all superior about what we do and how we dress, let me remind you that it was only my decision to become English that has got us where we are today.'

The old lady took this outburst on the chin. She was about to say something, but DeVere was way ahead of her.

'And before you say "that is no way to speak to your mother" let me tell you that you can't have it both ways. And it's time you learnt on which side your bread is buttered.'

Mrs Polouvička was dumbfounded by this tirade, but heard him out defiantly. She was not used to being spoken to in this way, but she could not allow her son to get the better of her. Yet she could not challenge the sentiment of his statement. She looked at him in silence for a moment, and searched his face.

'Bedrich,' she said gently, 'come into the light for a moment.'

She took his arm, and he allowed himself to be led towards the window where the old lady peered up at his face again as if she had never seen it before.

'Bedrich,' she said in quiet amazement, 'are you trying to grow a moustache?'

DeVere was saved from having to compose an equally humiliating ripost by the sound of voices in the hall. Sir Grafton Willoughby and Brigadier Lemington had arrived, and were readying their armaments on the big central table.

'Had a good shoot at your place the other day, Willy,' boomed the brigadier.

'You were lucky – there just don't seem to be as many birds as I remember rearing. I'm hoping for a better shoot today.'

'Well, if it's not up to scratch, I shall have a lot to say at the committee meeting this week.'

'What committee meeting is that?'

'Landowners Association – Field Sports' Sub-Committee.'

'Oh, yes. Where is it this year?'

'Here, of course. Always is.'

'Does DeVere know? I mean, he's new.'

'Must do. I've had my invitation,' said the brigadier.

The echoing voices of DeVere's two counsellors and

those of the other guns as they began to arrive reminded DeVere of another Grantleigh tradition which he had been enjoined to preserve. He went into the dining room, took a set of silver tumblers from a corner cupboard, filled them with sloe gin, and took them into the hall on a silver tray. This was a fancy way of 'drawing for drive' usually done with numbered pegs – for on the bottom of each tumbler was a number which would determine the position of each gun for the first drive. They would then move up two places each drive thereafter.

'Good morning, gentlemen,' said DeVere as he joined the shooting party in the hall and handed round the drinks, which were grabbed and gulped down without causing any apparent break in the conversation.

'I was just saying,' said the brigadier, 'that if I don't bag half a dozen pheasants today, I'll have something to say at the committee meeting next week.'

'What committee meeting is that?' asked DeVere.

'The one here, of course – the Shoot Committee.'

'Here? I don't know of any meeting here.'

DeVere was about to probe for more information, when Hawkins came in to announce that the beaters were lined up in a cordon, ready to go through the Holmwood shelter belts for the first drive, and that the guns had better get to Hardnip Fields fast if they were to benefit from any pheasants they put up. The shooting party seized their guns and filed out to the waiting vehicles in the forecourt. Only the brigadier found reason to linger.

'Can't remember what my number was,' he said, looking at his tumbler. 'I'd better have another of those sloe gins, just to check it.'

For much of her married life, Audrey had been a shooting widow. You didn't have to be a pheasant to hate Saturdays, since her involvement in the shoot was domestic and peripheral. She provided the soup-and-sandwich lunch at the sawmill for the guns, and then tea at the manor at twilight. But since Marton's death, she had also taken over its administration – that is to say, she had done nothing at all except send out the invitations to the annual meeting of the Field Sports' Sub-Committee. The names were listed in a file that had come over from the manor, with many other of Marton's personal things. One name which was not on the list was that of Richard DeVere, which was why he had received no notification of the meeting.

The meeting tended to be social rather than practical. All Audrey knew about shooting in practice was that it made a lot of noise which was deafening if you were anywhere near it, and irritating even if you were anywhere within earshot. Since she had moved to the lodge, she made a practice of asking Hawkins what time the guns could be expected in the vicinity of the lodge, and she would then arrange to be out. There was always the weekend shopping to be done, but it was more in search of refuge that Audrey came to be in Mrs Patterson's store that Saturday morning.

'According to your notice outside, potatoes are slashed, Mrs Patterson.'

'That's right, dear.'

'Then if you've got any that aren't slashed, I'll have five pounds of those.'

'Five pounds of potatoes coming up,' chirped Mrs Patterson, flinging the merchandise on to the scale, and reading the weight.

'Just over. All right?'

She never waited for an answer to this question in case it wasn't, but she chatted on in the hope that the fact that it was a good half pound overweight would go unnoticed.

'And two pounds of apples,' demanded Audrey.

Mrs Patterson was in a chatty mood this morning.

'I see old Arthur Smith's in the district again.'

Audrey looked blankly.

'You know – Arthur Smith, the tramp,' Mrs Patterson

went on.

'Oh, yes – more of an itinerant labourer than a tramp, wouldn't you say?' said Audrey.

'No, I wouldn't,' protested Mrs Patterson. 'Smelly Smith, the tramp, that's what I call him.'

She was examining the scales for an approximation of two pounds' weight in apples.

'Just over. All right? I expect he'll be down to see you at the manor.'

This was all it took to put Audrey off the scent on the matter of the excess weight of apples.

'I no longer live at the manor, Mrs Patterson. How many times do I have to tell you?' she asked with irritation.

'Sorry dear, I forgot,' lied Mrs Patterson. 'Let's see now – that's, er, seventy-four pence so far.'

'Honestly, Mrs Patterson, your prices.'

'It's the friendly service you're paying for, Mrs fforbes-Hamilton. Anything else?'

'I think I've just got enough for a pound of bananas.'

'A pound of bananas it is, then,' she said, heaving a hand of the things from a crate on the floor. 'I suppose Smelly Smith will be knocking at Mr DeVere's door then. On the scrounge, like,' she said as she weighed the bananas.

'I think that's too strong a word,' Audrey objected. 'We need all the casual labour we can get at this time of the year.'

'People like him spoil the look of the place – scruffy beggar.'

'Only because he needs looking after. We always used to send him on his way as clean as a new pin,' said Audrey.

'Wasting your time, if you ask me.'

'I wasn't asking you, Mrs Patterson. I regard it as going with the job.'

Mrs Patterson consulted the scales for an approximation of the weight of bananas.

'Just over. All right?'

Audrey did not protest.

'That's one pound, six pence in all, then,' said the greengrocer, expertly spinning a bag of bananas in her fingers.

'Oh, dear,' said Audrey, fumbling in her purse. 'I only seem to have a pound.' She slapped the note on the counter, and made her way to the door.

'What's this then?' protested Mrs Patterson.

'Just under, all right?' said Audrey smugly, as she left the shop.

When she got back to the lodge, the fabled tramp, Arthur Smith, had already got his feet under the table and his dirty old hat upon it. Brabinger had cooked him a meal which Arthur was finishing off in a flourish of gravy-soaked bread, while the old butler paced round him with his boots squeaking abominably.

The sight of this big man sitting in her kitchen surprised Audrey, not because she didn't expect him to be there or objected to him, but because he seemed strangely out of place. But having made him welcome, she realized almost immediately that what was out of place was not him, but her. He had been coming to Grantleigh for years, and against the setting of the manor – either in the big servants' hall or framed in the huge doorways, cap in hand or bumbling around the surrounding countryside – Arthur Smith constituted a very harmonious and natural picture. He even looked small – but here in the lodge, in her own little kitchen and standing at such close range that she could see the details of his craggy, unshaven, weatherbeaten face and feel dwarfed by his huge frame – his presence dominated the room. Furthermore, the smell emanating from his clothes, which you'd scarcely noticed in one of the big rooms at the manor, was overpowering.

Noticing at once that he was giving offence, Arthur made reference to the fact – what, in other circumstances, would have been called 'clearing the air'.

'Sorry about that,' he said in obsequious tones. 'I've just spent a couple of weeks slurry carting at Moneymore Park.'

'Oh, yes,' said Audrey casually as if the smell was the last thing on her mind. 'That's the Willoughby place, isn't it? How are things there?'

The question was not asked casually, for Audrey knew that Arthur Smith was the biggest and best-informed gossip-monger in the West Country. Indeed, it was said that this was the reason why she had no objection to his visits. That was one reason, true, but the fact that Arthur Smith was a Grantleigh tradition, almost an institution which she had grown up with, was enough to account for her tolerance and kindly disposition towards him. Brabinger was less so, and he, glad to hand over the job of entertaining the tramp to Audrey, left the room, his squeaky boots grating on Audrey's nerves. He was not at all interested in hanging about to hear how things were going at Moneymore.

'They're going to pot, I'm afraid,' confided the tramp to Audrey. 'It's Sir Grafton's new wife. They say she's bleeding him dry.'

'I don't think I heard that,' Audrey pretended to object.

'I'd be lucky to get a pig's blister out of them. Same at Mountford Hall in Hampshire where I helped with the tree planting. Mean as sin, there. Not like here at Grantleigh.'

'We've always done our best. I see you've eaten.'

'I've done very well, ma'am,' he said, getting up from the table. 'Show me a slurry cart, and I'll be starting work right away – it'll be just like the old days.'

Audrey turned solemn.

'No, Arthur,' she said ruefully, 'I'm afraid things aren't just like the old days. When you're ready for your supper, perhaps you'd like to call in at the manor.'

'I have – new bloke up there threw me out.'

Aha! Audrey had got something on DeVere now. Just what she was looking for!

'Did he, indeed? Well, you leave him to me.'

'Right-ho, Mrs fforbes-Hamilton. I'll be joining the toilers in the vineyard then. Thanks for lunch.'

With that he disappeared out through the back door, leaving his hat on the table. No sooner had he gone than Audrey saw it there, put on a rubber glove, grabbed the wooden washing tongs, picked up the offending article in its claws and dropped it in the pedal bin, followed by tongs and rubber glove.

'Who said you could feed him?' she asked Brabinger later that afternoon.

'We always used to at the manor,' stammered Brabinger.

'He's Mr DeVere's responsibility now. He'll be working for him, so he can feed him.' She began to unpack her shopping basket. 'Besides, I'm too busy at the moment. We've got the Landowners Association meeting at the weekend, and I've got all the paper work to do.'

Brabinger didn't like the sound of this. Years of experience of Audrey's moods had taught him that whenever she claimed to be 'busy', she tended to be a bit rancorous. He was offering no prizes for guessing who got the rough edge of her tongue. It was not the sort of mood which took kindly to squeaky boots on the feet of elderly retainers.

'Oh, do get yourself some new boots, Brabinger,' she barked as he left the room. 'That noise is driving me quite mad.'

'But these boots are new, madam – they'll settle down.'

'You've been saying that for the last year.'

Brabinger had come to regard Richard DeVere as an ally – somebody with whom he could share the burden of Audrey's line in invective. DeVere was a useful scapegoat because almost anything that went wrong in Audrey's life could, in some way, be blamed on him, which left Brabinger in the clear. What's more, it had become one of Brabinger's great pleasures in life to eavesdrop on their conversations, which often ended up as full-blown rows. It was one of these which was to provide his entertainment for the evening, when DeVere called round brandishing an empty folder the following day.

Audrey gave him a chilly reception.

'I'm glad you called round. I've got a bone to pick with you.'

'And I've got one to pick with you. What's all this about a local Landowners Association meeting on Friday?'

'It's only the Shooting Sub-Committee. We just sit around and talk about pheasant poaching.'

'Why haven't I been asked to this meeting?'

Audrey did not realize this till now. She had no ready answer.

'Because your name wasn't on the list, but you'd be most welcome,' she offered casually.

'The meeting's at the manor, isn't it?'

'Yes, of course.'

'I see, so you'd be inviting me to my own house?'

'Don't say you didn't know that. It's in the minutes for last year.'

'Is it? I looked out the Landowners Association file in the estate office, and look.' He opened his blue folder. It was empty.

'They can't be in two places at once, can they?' he pointed out.

'Are you accusing me of taking your files?'

'It isn't that so much, but before you go inviting all and sundry to my house, I think you could have asked me, that's all.'

'It isn't all and sundry. It's just you and me and Sir Grafton Willoughby and Brigadier Lemington from the nearby estates, and Hawkins our gamekeeper. The others always refuse and before you go lecturing me about how to behave, what about Arthur Smith?'

'Who the hell is Arthur Smith?'

'He's a tramp. A casual labourer. Somebody you threw

out this morning.'

'Threw out?'

'Neck and crop.'

'What – that tramp?'

'He may be a tramp to you, but to us he has always been a valuable member of the estate work force.'

'No stinking tramp is part of my work force. The least I ask of my staff is a regular wash.'

'He has a regular wash. Once a year to my knowledge. He goes up to the cottage hospital for a shower.'

'Oh, you can get a shower up there, can you?'

'I assume so. I expect it's only a joke, but they say that he just stands there under the sprinkler and shouts "fire".'

'You know a lot about him.'

'Of course I do. He comes here every year and helps with the slurry carting. In return we feed him, we let him sleep in the barns, we clean him up, and sometimes we give him one of Marton's old suits to see him on his way.'

'Well, don't let me stop you.'

'When I say "we", I mean "you". You can't expect me to feed him while he's doing your work. I think you'll find he has quite a personality.'

'Yes, I've smelt it.'

'And that's another thing. It's a bit overpowering in a house this size. At the manor his personality has got more room to move about.'

'Audrey, you don't honestly expect me to take him in?'

'If he has one failing, it's that he's a bit of a gossip. If he goes on from here to other big houses and talks of the shabby treatment he got at Grantleigh, your name will be mud the length and breadth of the county.'

'I'm used to that.'

'So you may be, but you'd be dragging the good name of Grantleigh down with you.'

'Well, if he has the gall to show up again, I'll bear that in mind.'

With that, he made his way to the door.

'Well, thanks for the lecture. Next time you want to throw a party in my house, just let me know.'

Audrey had hoped that that matter had been disposed of and would not come up again. Her panegyric on behalf of Arthur Smith, whilst deeply felt, was more of a way of changing the subject, for she realized at once that not inviting DeVere to the meeting was an appalling social gaffe which was not then put right by her inviting him to his own house. A little humility would not go amiss, she felt. And DeVere provided the opportunity.

'I'm sorry to have barged in like this over such a small thing. I know that you are extremely busy.'

'Oh, I wouldn't have said I was *extremely* busy, but pretty.' DeVere fixed her with an impish stare.

'I didn't say you were pretty,' he chortled.

Audrey glared at him.

'Get out,' she said.

Brabinger had overheard all this conversation up until the point where they left the drawing room and came into the hall, at which point he squeaked his way into the kitchen and closed the door.

Here he found Arthur Smith who had barged in as if he owned the place and was searching over the room for his hat. Even with Brabinger joining in the search, it had yielded nothing. Soon Audrey joined them in the room to see what the chatter and the banging of cupboard doors was all about.

'Mr Smith seems to have mislaid his hat, madam,' explained Brabinger.

Audrey wandered casually over to the sink side of the room, and as if by accident, trod on the pedal of the waste bin.

'Gracious me!' she exclaimed in bogus surprise, as she stared into the gaping maw of the pedal bin. 'It must have fallen in here.'

The tramp retrieved it eagerly, noticing the tongs lying alongside at the bottom of the bin.

'You're not chucking these out, are you?' he asked, grasping the tongs.

'Yes, I think they must have woodworm.'

'Mind if I have them? In my job you get one or two things you don't like to handle.'

Audrey shuddered at the thought of what such 'things' might be.

'Quite,' she said. 'Oh, about your meals. I've spoken to Mr DeVere and he says you'll be most welcome at the manor.'

Brabinger looked at her in amazement. From what he had heard of the conversation, no such thing had been said. She parried his gaze with a stern one of her own, directed at his squeaky feet.

'What did I tell you about those boots?' she asked with the tones of a final warning.

Now that he had been formally invited to the meeting, DeVere felt duty-bound to make his attendance worthwhile. He would not want to come to it with no more than an empty folder, and it was not his style to be left out of any discussion. What he needed, and now had time to indulge, was a crash course in shooting and what the committee would refer to as 'matters arising'. If poaching was to be the topic, as Audrey had intimated, poaching would be the subject he'd bone up on. That was why he was now up in the woods looking for Hawkins. Knowing that he was sometimes to be found around the release pens, DeVere had left his Range-Rover at the bottom of the track, and was treading ground which in normal circumstances would be used by Hawkins himself, pheasants or poachers. He was just approaching the release pens when a gun shot rang out from the nearby bushes and DeVere was propelled to the ground as frightened birds took to the air, squawking.

'All right, all right, let's have you,' yelled Hawkins scrambling out of the bushes. 'How many have you got? I'll teach you to poach in broad daylight.'

It was not until DeVere found himself staring down the business end of a shotgun that Hawkins realized who he was.

'Oh, beg your pardon, sir.'

'What the devil did you shoot at me for? I could have been killed.'

'I didn't shoot at you, sir.'

'I heard a shot, dammit,' said DeVere, getting up and brushing himself down.

'Alarm gun, sir,' said Hawkins, pointing to the tripwire DeVere had just been over.

DeVere hadn't seen such a device before, and was intrigued by it. Hawkins demonstrated the mechanism with some pride. It was a simple tripwire connected to a rod, which was dug into the ground on one side. Contact with the tripwire triggered a firing pin which set off a cartridge. The lead shot fired harmlessly into the ground, but it was the noise which had the required effect.

'If it doesn't scare poachers off, it tells me someone's snooping about, but of course it doesn't tell me *who*,' said Hawkins, as he reset the alarm gun with another cartridge and trailed the tripwire round behind DeVere and tightened it.

'I'm not snooping,' said DeVere. 'I came to see you. It's poaching I want to talk to you about, as a matter of fact.'

'There's a lot of it about, sir. That I know.'

'Could you come down to the office and tell me about it? I want to get a report together.'

'Right away, sir.'

Hawkins turned and set off back along the track which led deeper into the wood.

'Where are you going?' asked DeVere.

'Short cut across Hardnip Fields, sir.'

'Don't bother. I've got the car here,' said DeVere, pointing the way he had come. He set off towards it. There was another gun shot and DeVere was on the ground again and birds took to the air. DeVere swore as the tripwire zinged at him mockingly.

It was a tenet in Audrey's somewhat egocentric philosophy that more important than that things should be done was that they should be *seen* to be done. By the time silence had reigned for over an hour after supper *à deux* at the lodge, it became apparent that Marjory had been invited for the evening merely to watch Audrey do all the paper work in preparation for the shoot meeting. She could bear the silence no more and protested.

'Come round for a chinwag, that's what you said.'

'There's nothing to stop you wagging your chin if you really want to,' said Audrey facetiously. 'I'm sorry, but when I address this meeting, I want to be sure of my facts and figures. Now, I know exactly how many we reared, and how many we released last autumn. What we need to know is how many were shot so far this season, and add to it the number that are left. Then the difference between the two figures will be how many have been poached.'

'How do you know how many were shot?'

'It's all in here,' said Audrey, picking up a leather-bound ledger from her folder. 'The game book.'

She opened it, and her smug smile faded. The book was empty. Not a single entry was in it.

'Oh, those poor dead pheasants gave their all, and without so much as a memorial.'

'Maybe the shooters didn't hit anything.'

'All that banging in the woods all winter. They must have hit something, and it should all be entered up in here, even if it's only a tree. Honestly, DeVere is hopeless.'

'How could he have entered anything up if you had the book?'

'That has nothing to do with it. That's his second bit of negligence this week.'

'What was the other thing?'

'The small matter of Arthur Smith.'

'Oh, Arthur.'

'I just can't make him see that he may be an eyesore, but he's a good worker, and he is DeVere's responsibility.'

The sentiment rang bells in what Marjory loosely called 'her mind' – a poem by Wordsworth about a lakeland tramp of Arthur Smith's ilk, that she had learnt at school. Lines came back to her.

''Tis Nature's law
But none the meanest of creative things
Of forms created the most vile and brute
The dullest or most noxious should exist
Divorced from good. . . .'

'That rings a bell.'

'Wordsworth. That poem about the old beggar we learnt for elocution at school. Remember?'

'Yes, I remember it well.'

It was on the tip of her tongue, but try as she might, she couldn't propel it any further.

'How does it go on?'

'Which man is born to sink howe'er depressed
So low as to be scorned without a sin,
Without offence to God cast out from view . . .'

The cue opened the floodgates of Audrey's memory.

'. . . like the dry remnant of a garden flower,' they chorused triumphantly. Their recitation was interrupted by Brabinger who came to explain that DeVere had thrown Arthur Smith out of the manor again, and that the tramp had arrived on the lodge doorstep, expecting to be fed.

The news exasperated Audrey, but she reacted stoically.

'Excuse me, Marjory,' she said, getting up. 'Our dried

remnant needs watering.'

She went into the kitchen where she found Arthur Smith waiting, hat in hand, at the door.

'Mr Smith, I can't apologize enough for the shabby treatment you're getting at the manor.'

'Sorry to be a nuisance, ma'am,' said Arthur. 'Not at all. I feel responsible,' she said benevolently, as she searched the fridge. 'Brabinger, there's a steak in here,' she went on.

'That was for the dog, ma'am.'

'Then let Mr Smith have it. Bertie can have the liver, and I'll send the bill to Mr DeVere,' said Audrey, resolving the whole situation at a stroke.

Arthur was overwhelmed.

'I wish every estate was like this, ma'am,' he said. 'Harborough Hall, Beauminster Towers, Moneymore – all the same – no matter how much work I put in, I'm lucky to get a pig's blister. But here, well, it's like coming home. Bless you for it, ma'am.'

This was music to Audrey's ears, for she knew that such glowing reports of her hospitality would be spread from Salisbury to Land's End – anywhere Arthur Smith's itinerary took him.

'It's the least we can do. After all, "which man is born to sink howe'er depressed so low as to be viewed without offence – um – to scorn, cast out – of sin – ".'

Her memory of the apposite quotation floundered.

'Would you like it fried or grilled?' she added as if it was the final line of her quotation.

And so it was, that for the next few days Arthur Smith came to the lodge for all his meals, much to Brabinger's disgust. But in Audrey, it reawakened the old spirit of patronage which hadn't had a good airing since she'd left the manor. There was a time when she dominated the whole neighbourhood and everybody in it, but now it seemed they had sworn allegiance to her successor. Arthur Smith was the last remaining outlet for her *noblesse oblige*. Hence the lecture Brabinger got whenever he rebelled against the presence of their visitor. Audrey had just returned from a shopping trip to Marlbury and was complaining that you couldn't get twirly stick barley sugar any more and that AA patrol men didn't salute, when Brabinger brought the subject up.

'How much longer do we have to put up with him?' he grumbled. 'Why do you have to feed him? In the old days we just used to give the casuals a Somerset clanger.'

A 'Somerset clanger' was a suet roll with meat at one end and sweet at the other which labourers took to the fields.

'They used to wrap them up and put them under cow pats to keep warm,' he added for Audrey's enlightenment.

'How quaint,' she said with disgust and guided him back to the subject of Arthur Smith.

'I know you don't like him here,' she acknowledged. 'But it's only for a week. And I think you could be more Christian.'

'Sometimes it isn't easy, madam.'

'Of course it isn't easy, Brabinger. There wouldn't be any virtue in it if it was. Nobody *likes* having beggars around the place, but we should be thankful we are in a position to look after the poor and needy.'

'I'm sure I'm most grateful, madam,' the old man muttered. He'd been in a bad mood all day – it had started badly when he couldn't find his favourite pair of boots, and got worse from then on.

'Don't be like that, Brabinger. We're very lucky. Ever since the welfare state, there simply aren't enough beggars to go round. We should consider it a privilege to have Arthur here with us – to be able to clean him up and give him clothes.'

Brabinger agreed, but only because that's what he was paid to do.

Audrey continued, 'Unfortunately, we are not in a position to be so charitable this year. The only suits in this house are yours.'

'You're not asking me to donate one of my suits, madam?' quailed the old retainer.

'Gracious, no. I wouldn't dream of it.'

In the last few days they had not had many conversations which had not been interrupted by the arrival of Smith expecting another meal – and this was no exception. What was different about his arrival this time was the familiar squeak which entered with him. Brabinger stared at the tramp's footwear in disbelief.

'Those are my boots,' he yelled in anguish.

'They're not. They're mine,' said the tramp. 'Mrs fforbes-Hamilton gave them to me.'

Brabinger turned round to look at Audrey for confirmation of this theft, but she was no longer in the room. Within seconds, she was back in the room carrying a small, brown, paper package.

'Oh, I completely forgot, Brabinger. I bought something for you in Marlbury today.'

She handed him the package which he opened suspiciously. It was a pair of boots identical to the ones which she had given to the tramp – except in one respect which Audrey was at pains to demonstrate.

They were squeakless.

At about the same time that Arthur was at the lodge, claiming that DeVere had thrown him out again, DeVere was sitting at home, wondering whether perhaps that was what he should have done. In fact, he had given instructions for the tramp to be fed and watered and housed in the manor's servants' wing. After all, the fellow was working for him. He had capitulated totally on the matter of the tramp, purely to appease Audrey, who was, at that moment, serving the vagrant's second meal of the evening. It worried DeVere all night that he'd been so easily persuaded to ditch his principles which upheld a work philosophy that did not include idle tramps.

Hence, he was not pleased to find this particular tramp knocking on the drawing room french window before breakfast the following morning.

'Nasty morning,' said the tramp.

'Is it? Nobody tells me anything,' snarled DeVere sarcastically.

The tramp strode confidently into the room, and took in his surroundings.

'You've got this room looking nice,' he said. 'In the old days, there was a chesterfield *here*, and a cabinet *there* . . .'

'I prefer things as they are,' sneered DeVere, too amazed at the man's gall to pitch straight into him. 'I'd also prefer it if you'd go and get on with your work.'

The tramp ignored the suggestion and continued to look round.

'Pity about her over there,' he mused, nodding towards the lodge. 'She used to be so kind, and suddenly she doesn't know me. I'd be lucky to get a pig's blister out of her.'

He fixed DeVere with a suggestive leer and nudged him.

'Shame you and she don't get on – know what I mean?'

DeVere's patience ran out there and then.

'Have you had your breakfast?' he asked, testily.

'Thank you, yes.'

'Then there's nothing to keep you in the house, so would you mind leaving, because I haven't.'

'I can tell you what you're getting, sir, because I've brought it,' boasted the tramp, whereupon he thrust his grubby, mittened hands into his pockets and pulled out a couple of muck-spattered eggs.

'There,' said Smith, holding them up in his dirty palms. 'Fresh eggs, collected with my own fair hands.'

'And what is the meaning of this?' demanded Mrs Polouvička, invading the supposed sanctuary of DeVere's private office that evening, brandishing a sock. DeVere, who was arranging the table and chairs for the Shoot Sub-Committee meeting, gave the object a cursory glance and identified it. It was not only caked in dirt, and full of holes, but it appeared to hum and wriggle a bit.

'How does a son of mine get his sock in this condition?' demanded the old lady.

'Whcrc did you find it?'

'In your bathroom. And what's more, the bath is disgusting. I've never seen such a black ring.'

DeVere knew at once who the donor was.

'He's got a cheek, that man.'

'What man?'

'Smith. Well, I don't mind feeding him, I don't mind putting him up in the servants' wing. Yes, I did give him permission to have a bath, but not in my bathroom.'

'You should have thrown him out.'

'I couldn't throw him out. I've been safeguarding the reputation of the estate, apparently. According to Audrey, that freeloader is our self-appointed public relations officer.'

He'd no sooner spoken than the self-appointed public relations officer appeared, framed in the doorway, looking more presentable than he had ever been seen before. He was not only clean and groomed, and gleaming with after-shave lotion – DeVere's – he was also wearing a shirt and tie and a pinstripe suit. It didn't exactly fit, but, apart from his grubby hat, he presented a not unsightly picture, with Brabinger's squeaky boots providing the soundtrack.

'Got to be on my way, Mr DeVere,' he said.

'So the suit fitted all right?' asked DeVere, trying to keep up the façade of eternal friendship. But the sight of the suit was too much for Mrs Polouvička.

'That's your best suit, Bedrich.'

'It was in nineteen sixty-three, yes, and he's welcome to it.'

'Most generous, I'm sure,' said the tramp. 'Good-day, and thank you for your hospitality.'

'And thank you for all your hard work,' returned DeVere.

'It was nothing. A clean shirt, a new suit and a few drinks and cigars and a full stomach mean more than money to me.'

The mention of money stirred qualms within DeVere, and a reflex action sent his hand to his wallet. He was not feeling in a particularly generous mood, it was just that he was anxious to do anything to precipitate the tramp's departure, even if it meant parting with some money.

He was not a mean man. After all, Smith had been working for him for the week, and a few pounds was a small price to pay for the public relations value, which he would undoubtedly do on behalf of the estate in his subsequent peregrinations. Arthur Smith read his thoughts.

'No, no, I couldn't,' he insisted with a gesture of refusal.

'I insist,' said DeVere, 'I'd hate anybody to think we don't pay the rate for the job.'

Arthur Smith pressed his point home.

'But it was only ten hours a day for seven days. I mean, what's a pound an hour between friends?'

DeVere was not splashing out.

'Let's say fifty pounds,' he said, counting out the bank notes from his wallet.

'If you insist,' said Arthur, and the bank notes vanished almost before they had left the wallet. 'It's been a good week and I shall speak highly of Grantleigh wherever I go. Always have, always will,' he said.

He turned and made for the door, turned round and lingered a moment savouring the smoke from DeVere's cigar. Anxious not to delay his departure, DeVere took the hint and slipped a couple of cigars into his top pocket.

'There. And if ever you're passing this way again – keep passing.'

The tramp opened the door, and would have gone through it, but for Mrs Polouvička's intervention.

'Mr Smith,' she challenged, sternly, 'I'd hate you to go without something from me, too.' She held out the sock, as if making him a present of it. The tramp was equally gracious.

'Very kind of you, I'm sure, ma'am,' he said, 'but you've been so generous – I couldn't take another thing.'

With that, he left the room.

'Oh, well,' said Mrs Polouvička, hurling the sock into the fire, 'it's the thought that counts – as the old English saying goes.'

Stepping out into the chill night, Arthur counted his money by the light of the moon, and then thrust the notes into an already bulging wallet, and made his way down the drive to the lodge.

Audrey was gathering up her papers and files in preparation for the meeting at the manor when he called.

'Gracious, I didn't recognize you in that suit,' she said, as she opened the door to him. 'Who gave you that?'

'Mr DeVere.'

Well, that was *something* she thought, but pathetically mean for a man of DeVere's means.

'I did have to remind him of our long-standing arrangement,' she said.

'He only gave it to me on condition that I went away.'

'Oh dear, so you're off, are you? Well, thank you for all your hard work.'

'And thank you for your hospitality, ma'am. Much more rewarding than mere money.'

The mention of money stirred feelings in her. They were not those which DeVere had felt, for to him, money was a commodity to be protected. Her instinct, on the other hand, was that money was a commodity to be given away in such circumstances as these. She went into the hall, and rummaged in her handbag, and returned to the door.

'I'm sorry it can't be as much as in the old days,' she said.

'Will fifty be enough?'

'No, no. I couldn't, madam. Well, if you insist,' said Arthur holding out his hand.

'There,' said Audrey, cheerfully, pressing a fifty-pence coin into his hand. 'And good luck to you.'

No sooner had Smith made off into the night, grumbling at this pittance, than the lodge door opened again, and Audrey emerged and stormed down the drive to the manor, muttering to herself. Hers were not the movements of one who is simply going to a routine meeting. She had been rehearsing something – but at the same time, working herself into a frenzy on the matter of Arthur Smith. Locating the object of her fury in his private office, pouring over the shoot accounts, she gave vent to her feelings.

'So you gave him a suit?'

'Yes, I gave him a suit,' said DeVere without looking up.

'Bully for you. A multi-millionaire, owner of a nationwide grocery empire, and all you gave him was a mouldy old suit. Whereas I, a poor widow . . .'

'Actually, it was a very good suit. For a tramp.'

'He may be an old tramp, but that doesn't mean that you can throw him out like a dry remnant of a garden flower.'

DeVere was startled by this lyrical flourish and looked up.

'A what?'

'Do you ever read poetry?'

'No. Fiction mainly, judging by these balance sheets of yours.'

'That was Wordsworth.'

'Oh, he did these accounts, did he?'

'The poet, Wordsworth. Reminding us of our duty towards the poor. Smith should not be viewed as a dry remnant of a garden flower, but should be looked after by people like us.'

DeVere saw no reason for this lecture, and rose to his defence.

'Your dry remnant has certainly blossomed a bit since he's been here, let me tell you,' DeVere protested. 'I fed him, didn't I? Housed him, let him have a bath – my bath, as it happens – gave him cigars. What more do you want?'

'Oh.'

Audrey was dumbstruck for a moment.

'How could you have been feeding him? What do you think I've been doing all this week?'

It didn't take a brain like DeVere's a second to grasp the whole situation.

'Crafty devil,' he exclaimed. 'He's been playing us off against each other. I should have given him a job in head office.' He roared with laughter.

Audrey did not.

'It's no laughing matter, Richard. I gave him some money.'

'So did I. But what the hell? He's been making himself useful.'

The argument went into abeyance, to make way for the exchange of pleasantries which went with the arrival of Sir Grafton Willoughby. In one hand he carried his papers for the meeting and in the other a whisky bottle.

'What's that for?' asked DeVere.

'Thought it might see us through the meeting,' said Sir Grafton.

DeVere pointed to a selection of bottles already on the table.

'No need,' he said.

'Oh, the rumours aren't true then?'

'What rumours?'

'That the place had become a sort of temperance hall.'

'Nonsense.'

'Oh well, I'm relieved it's not true.'

'What's not true?' said Audrey.

'Oh, nothing, really. But I just heard a buzz that one

would be lucky to get a pig's blister out of this estate these days.'

'Who told you that?' asked DeVere.

'One of my casual labourers. Sort of tramp fellow – been working on my estate. Comes every year.'

'Really,' said DeVere with increasing interest. 'Does he work strange hours, by any chance?'

'What if he does?' asked Sir Grafton. 'We only have to house and feed him, and he always refuses to be paid. Mind you, I slip him the odd fifty.'

'Pence?' asked Audrey.

'Pounds.'

The door opened again to admit Brigadier Lemington.

'Come in, brigadier,' welcomed DeVere. 'Join the party.'

'Party, is it? Well, that's not what I expected,' said the brigadier.

'Drink?'

'Yes, I have, thanks,' said the brigadier, waving a hip flask. DeVere divined the significance of the brigadier bringing his own hooch.

'Have you heard that the largesse of Grantleigh has been lacking in some way?' he asked.

'Well yes, actually,' admitted the brigadier. 'Chap working on my estate said it had suddenly degenerated into a pig's blister.'

The story was the same. The reputation of Grantleigh had been spreading, it seemed, and nobody here was in any doubt as to the identity of the carrier.

'And he told me the same about you two,' said Audrey.

The two landowners dismissed their new-found reputation with the flippancy the matter deserved. What's more, they bore the loss of their respective fifty pounds stoically, deeming it an occupational hazard. But not so Audrey. She was working out exactly how Arthur Smith had been spending his week.

'If he was working for you two, how could he have been

working for us here?' she figured.

'He wasn't,' DeVere asserted. 'Couldn't have had time. He was just going round having meals with everybody. Not bad, eh? Never does any work – six meals a day in the best houses in the county – what a life – and for a hundred and fifty pounds a week.'

'. . . and fifty pence,' Audrey reminded him.

The men laughed. The clock struck, and DeVere called the meeting to order. Item one was game poaching.

'Hawkins isn't here,' observed Audrey, noticing his absence.

'He's doing a job for me,' said DeVere. 'Now . . .'

DeVere took immediate control of the meeting. This startled the other three for a moment, since DeVere was undoubtedly the junior member present. Yet there was something about his commanding manner which was irresistable, and they allowed him to take over. Within minutes, it was perfectly clear that DeVere knew much more about the matter in hand than they did. He regaled the meeting with an interesting set of facts and figures, and it was clear that he had furnished himself with a full account of poaching, figures distilled from the relevant police files from four areas covering theirs and other neighbouring estates. Not only that, but he'd also drawn a conclusion from the information, which he proceeded to explain in detail without pausing for breath, except to silence any interjections.

He'd worked out that the poaching pattern was the same year in and year out, and nobody had yet tumbled to it. The incidents of prowlers reported and shots heard showed similarities which indicated that the poachers or poacher had a well-established method. Manifestations of poaching would occur at night on three or four consecutive days – long enough for the landowner to look to his security, but not long enough for the poachers to fall foul of it. They would be on their way then. Furthermore, the incidents seemed to happen in one place at a time, indicating that it was the same operator, and looking at maps of the West Country in relation to the reports at their disposal, one could see that the outbreaks were moving from estate to estate, from east to west.

'And, I have reason to believe that security should be stepped up on this estate at the moment, since we must be next in line, so I can't afford to have Hawkins drop his guard.'

The other two landowners had nothing to add to the conversation, except expressions of amazement.

'Good grief.'

'By jove!'

'Great powers!'

'Deuced clever, what!'

'Well, bless my pants!'

Until silence reigned save for the swallowing of hard liquor. It was broken by Audrey.

'That east-west itinerary is familiar,' she mused. 'I've heard it before.'

'It's a professional job, all right,' said DeVere knowingly. 'But that doesn't mean to say that our man *looks* like a professional.'

The brigadier was flabbergasted and said, 'Well, I'll be jiggered. Do you mean that the man we're looking for is . . .?'

'We have no proof at this moment,' said DeVere, 'but we will.'

The brigadier tried to subdue his shock with another large gulp of whisky. Suddenly there was a loud explosion in the distance, which echoed across the estate.

'My God, good stuff, this,' said the brigadier bringing the glass down as the explosion sang in his ears.

'Did we say something to offend them?' offered Sir Grafton, realizing that they were suddenly alone in the room. Audrey and DeVere had jumped up and dashed out of the house. They drove up the home farm track, abandoned the Range-Rover as soon as it might have been within earshot of the woods, and they were soon creeping up the feed-ride towards the release pen. There was no doubt in Audrey's mind who they were pursuing – she could hear the squeaking of boots.

Arthur Smith had been driving his mini-van load of dead pheasants through the woods, picking his way carefully on dipped headlights. He was congratulating himself on a good week's haul, and counting up what he'd make on the cargo when he delivered it to the London butcher for whom he was the regular supplier. It was just a few yards to the edge of the wood, then on to the farm track and out on the eastern drive of the estate – and he would be off.

He edged the van on to the feed-ride and was easing down the slope when he drove into the tripwire. The alarm gun sounded and the wire wound round his axle and snarled his wheel. At the sound of the explosion of the gun shot, he leapt out in panic thinking he was being sniped by a crazed lunatic of a gamekeeper, and he hid behind a tree. From this vantage point, he was able to size up the situation, and, realizing he was still alone, he emerged, albeit cautiously, to disentangle the tripwire. But it took longer to free his wheel then it took Hawkins to arrive at the feed-ride from one direction, and DeVere and Audrey from the other. Smith was cornered. But in the darkness he could not identify who the other people were.

'Is this the road to Lyme Regis?' he asked innocently – but then he recognized DeVere and ran off in the other direction, only to be menaced by Hawkins with his gun.

'Hold it there,' yelled Hawkins. He motioned Smith to turn and face DeVere.

'All right, Smith. What have you got in this van?'

'No birds in there, sir. Honest,' quavered the poacher.

DeVere peered into the darkness at the back of the van, but there was enough light to make out the shape of several hundred dead pheasants.

'What's this then? Mass suicide?' he ventured.

'Pheasants get depressed, sir,' the tramp risked.

DeVere sighed and motioned Hawkins.

'Get those pheasants out of there and see this man off the estate, would you?' he said, and turned to leave the scene.

'If you say so, sir, but if . . .'

'I do say so,' DeVere snapped. He turned to Audrey. 'I don't think we'll see your tramp around here again, do you?'

Audrey was appalled by the leniency of his attitude.

'Are you going to let him go?' she gasped.

'It'll be cheaper and less trouble.'

'Aren't you going to arrest him?' she said appalled. 'I mean, he's got fifty pence of mine – and Brabinger's boots.'

'I'll see you're compensated,' said DeVere walking away. Audrey followed him and tried to draw him back to the scene of the crime.

'But that man's a common criminal,' she pointed out.

'Oh, I wouldn't call him that.'

'Well, I don't know what you would call him then,' Audrey protested.

DeVere patronized her with a patient look – that of a man with bigger things to think about and with enormous reserves of goodwill.

'Don't you?' he replied. 'How about a "dry remnant of a garden flower"?'

4

The lesson for Audrey of DeVere's act of clemency was that she did not have an exclusive monopoly on his goodwill. She had benefitted from it countless times, but the incident showed that he gave her no priority – that as candidates for his generosity, she and the tramp were on a par. If the revelation of this softer side to his nature came as a shock, it was nothing compared with the impact of her discovery that he was also a connoisseur of fine arts.

DeVere was a passionate lover of china and porcelain, and the manor served as an appropriate backdrop to his priceless collection – Rockingham, Coalport, Sèvres, Limoges among them.

In all old houses such as the manor, there are areas of definite male and female influence. Foremost among the rooms on the distaff side was the tea-room. With its colourful wallpaper, curtains and French furniture, it was more decoratively appointed than, say, the library or the billiard room or the smoking room, which tended to be male sancturies and which were appropriately dowdy. But the tea-room at the manor had lost none of its feminine charm due to the encumbency of Richard DeVere. Indeed, it had been enhanced, for here were cabinets full of beautiful shapes and colours.

Audrey had been invited to the manor one morning to inspect a new acquisition. It was her first visit to the rooms since the takeover. She made her knowledgeable identification of the pieces sound like an on-site inventory which DeVere found impressive, though her voice betrayed a hint of nostalgia and envy.

'You seem to know a lot about china,' DeVere complimented her.

'I grew up with the best. I can remember a time when the family still used the handpainted Italian Majolica dinner service. Imagine parting your spinach and finding 'The Rape of the Sabine Women' going on underneath.'

DeVere did.

'Most unsettling.'

'And I remember my Great Uncle Peveril drinking from a Sèvres cup when he had his heart attack,' Audrey went on.

'He died?'

'Worse. It ruined the set.'

DeVere understood that and said so, though Audrey cast doubt on it.

'How could you understand?'

'Because my collection is my one pride and joy. There was a time, you know, when I had nothing. In the early days, my mother's taste in china wasn't exactly discerning.'

'Plaster ducks up the wall, was it?'

'Not that bad. No, it was those little wizened Arab faces staring down at us out of the walls. We've come a long way since then,' he added as he put his new acquisition down on one of the display cabinets, and began to unwrap it.

The exposed contents drew a gasp of admiration from Audrey. It was a vase – Egyptian – and she dated it somewhere between antique and prehistoric.

'What do you think?' said its proud owner.

'Why, it's beautiful. You could pay forty thousand pounds for something like that these days.'

'I did.'

'Worth every penny, if you know what that is,' said Audrey, as she took the piece and chose a prominent place for it on top of another display cabinet, between a Dresden comport and a Doulton *jardinière*.

'Be careful,' warned DeVere nervously.

'Scared I might drop it? Anyway, it's you who should be careful.'

'Why?'

'Security. You've got thousands of pounds worth of priceless pieces in here. Anyone could just walk in and help themselves.'

'Perhaps you're right. I'll have a word with the local police.'

The door opened, and Mrs Polouvička marched in, very cross at having found her son in the last place she would have thought of looking. But the idea of his sneaking off to this remote corner of the house with Audrey pleased her.

'I've just been admiring Richard's latest acquisition,' Audrey explained to pre-empt her insinuations.

'Oh, what's he wasting his pocket money on now?' scoffed the old lady. DeVere pointed, and his mother inspected the Egyptian vase with acute distaste.

'This jug?'

'Vase, mother.'

'It's chipped.'

'It's thousands of years old, Mrs Poo,' said Audrey. 'It's worth a lot of money.'

'Oh, I doubt it,' she insisted. 'It's probably second-hand.'

Audrey's enthusiasm for DeVere's collection was not as boundless as she had made out. She viewed it with envy in the perspective of her own collection, now sold save for one obese Buddha figure which Marton had brought back from India. Nobody wanted him, and he was the sole occupant of her own display cabinet at the lodge, where all that was left of any treasures were the shapes of their bases ringing the green baize like a scorched lawn. The bloated figure stared out at her through the glass, with a mocking glint in his eye.

He seemed to symbolize her predicament. He was just another of those things she was reduced to. It was the story of her life – reduced to living in a little house, reduced to one servant – and he away at this moment – deserted by friends, deserted even by her possessions. It was, therefore, a simple relief to get a visit from her one loyal friend, Marjory – a joy which turned to ashes when it became clear that Marjory had simply called in to say good-bye.

'Where are you going?'

'I'm producing the WI play this year, so I thought I'd do a week's stage-craft course at the art centre.'

'But that means that you won't be calling round for a whole week.'

'No. It's a residential course. We're doing "Anthony and Cleopatra".'

'I see. They're more important to you than me, are they? Well, off you go then and enjoy yourself,' Audrey said sulkily.

Marjory wished she hadn't bothered to call in.

'Don't be like that,' she said. 'I'll be back before you realize I've gone.'

'But I'll miss you,' Audrey whined. 'I'll be lonely.'

'Rubbish. You'll have lots of friends calling in.'

'They don't call in now.'

'You can't blame them. All you ever do is boss them about.'

'Are you saying I'm bossy?' Audrey accused her.

'Yes, I am,' Marjory affirmed.

'I am not bossy, so don't tell me I am.'

They argued the matter for a moment, until Audrey changed the subject.

'The point is, I'll be lonely with you gone,' she said.

'Oh, you don't know what loneliness is. You should hear Mrs Poo on the subject.'

Mrs Polouvička on the subject of loneliness had been a revelation to Marjory. Life in the household of Richard

DeVere in London had condemned her to weeks on her own while he was doing business all over the world. It had almost reached chronic proportions, and she was apparently reduced to searching the Yellow Pages for workmen to come and measure the house and give estimates for double glazing, new carpets and kitchen fittings and the like.

Audrey listened with interest.

'She had no intention of having any work actually carried out, but she just used to do it to get the company,' Marjory reported.

This little tale of human tragedy did little to improve Audrey's resentment of her pending imminent abandonment by Marjory. It was a matter of getting the parting over.

'Must go,' said Marjory. 'I've got to see Mrs Poo.'

'What about?'

'She promised to look after my yoghurt while I'm away,' waving the jar of the white rampant substance in Audrey's face.

Marjory went into the hall and picked up her holdalls.

'What have you got there?' demanded Audrey, following her out.

'Oh, just a few props and things for the production. We're supposed to use our imaginations and activate our subconscious.'

Audrey opened the door.

'Don't I get a kiss?' she said. The two kissed the air beside the other's ear.

'Good-bye,' said Marjory, 'I'll miss you.'

'You just did,' confirmed Audrey, indicating the air space at the side of her head.

'If I'd known I'd had Fort Knox on my patch, I'd have done something about it long ago,' whimpered Police Constable Peaslake of the Marlbury station, who had come to the manor to advise Richard DeVere on the security of his collection.

'Then what would you have done?' said DeVere.

'Put up a big sign saying "Priceless china collection. Keep out".'

'Is that the best you can do? I thought you were the crime prevention officer.'

'I am, sir. Why do you ask?'

'I thought I saw you on point duty last week.'

'I'm also head of traffic division, sir. Now, what you've got here is a security problem.'

DeVere could not conceal a note of irritation in his voice.

'That's why I sent for you.'

The constable produced a thick bundle of pamphlets and dumped them on the table.

'These may be the answer,' he said.

DeVere looked at the bundle.

'Yes, I could pile them up behind the door, couldn't I?' he said.

'You could, sir, or you could sit in here all day guarding it yourself.' He took in his surroundings. 'These are just cups and saucers, are they, sir?'

'Not just cups and saucers.'

'Oh, no, I see you have some plates as well. In here you'll find details of alarm systems, electrical fences and so forth.'

'I don't want to live in a prison camp.'

'Maybe you should have a direct line to our head of CID.'

'Good idea. I'll talk to him some time.'

'You are talking to him, sir. Don't worry, we'll make things so secure that not even you can get in.'

DeVere did not suffer fools gladly, and this was a fool.

'Look, I don't think we're getting very far,' he said. 'Nothing personal, but I think I'd better speak to the senior officer at your station.'

The constable eyed him smugly, and swayed back and forth on the balls of his feet.

'I see,' said DeVere, 'you *are* the senior officer at your station.'

Audrey began to feel lonely and neglected almost as soon as Marjory was out of the house. She realized instantly that she had nothing to look forward to for a whole week. Not even Brabinger's fawning tones to relieve the silence.

As time went by, she brooded on the fact that if all that she had to look forward to were visits from Marjory, then there wasn't a great deal to live for.

On the second day of despondency, Audrey realized that it was just not like her to let little things get her down. What had happened to her sense of fun – her sense of adventure, not to mention her courage in the face of adversity on which she prided herself? That day, she recognized that she had to take herself in hand and *do* something.

On the third day, she took a long, hard look at herself, and when she found herself sitting one morning on the sofa with nothing better to do than pop the bubbles in a polythene wrapping, she realized that the time had come to act. What was it Mrs Polouvička used to do in the circumstances?

She picked up the classified telephone directory and dialled a number. Within three minutes she had an appointment with the Cosyseal Double Glazing Company to measure windows up for a free estimate. Within six, she had arranged a visit from Modofit Designs with a view to having an estimate for a new kitchen. Within fifteen minutes, Sleepytime Bedrooms Limited and the Loft Insulation Company had got her down for two o'clock on Thursday, and by two o'clock on the Thursday, tradesmens vans, offering all manner of services from porch installations to security systems, were shuttling between Marlbury and Grantleigh in a steady stream. The lodge was suddenly receiving more visitors than it had seen in many a long day.

Audrey's wheeze at the lodge would have gone unnoticed were it not for an event at the manor which caused questions to be asked. The Egyptian vase, DeVere's prize possession, was stolen. One day it was there, the next it was gone. And anyone who happened to be passing the tea-room that morning would have been in no doubt as to how DeVere, normally the most placid of men, felt about it. He was ranting and banging his fists on the table until the china all round him began to tinkle and jump up and down in its cabinets, and Police Constable Peaslake began to quiver in his boots.

'I wanted a security system installed straight away. Now look what's happened,' he bawled.

'I'm sorry, sir, but the security people said they'd tie it in with another job they've got just up the road. When did you last see the vase?' asked Peaslake, affecting a dispassionate formality by way of dodging the blame.

'When you were here last. It was new.'

'New? Then it must have been an inside job'

'How do you work that out?'

'Can't be many people who even knew it was here. Who else lives here apart from your staff?'

'Just my mother.'

'Better talk to her,' said Peaslake, writing in his notebook. 'What is her full name?'

'Maria Jaroslava Vladimira Martinka Polouvička,' deVere rattled. The constable's pencil broke in the attempt to commit that to paper.

'I think we can rule her out,' he said.

'I should hope so. I don't want her thinking this place is a target for villains.'

The policeman put his notebook away and sighed.

'I think this'll be easy, sir,' he suggested.

'Well, what are you going to do?'

'Wait.'

'Yes, that sounds easy enough,' DeVere said with evident exasperation, by way of inviting further explanation.

'It's somebody local,' said Peaslake confidently. 'And they always give themselves away. We just have to watch out for somebody around here who seems to be spending more money than they've got.'

'It'll cost you,' the double-glazing fitter said to Audrey, shaking his head despairingly at the gothic-shaped windows of the lodge. For once, that did not bother Audrey.

'Money no object,' she said, breezily. 'But I want the glass to fit the mullions. I don't want you knocking the stonework around to fit the glass.'

The lodge was full of tradesmen all busying themselves with tape measures, rulers, set-squares, graph paper, notebooks full of geometrical shapes and calculations, and brochures. Audrey was in her element.

'Follow me, Kitchen,' she commanded. A man in a brown coat detached himself from the group and obliged, following her into the kitchen.

'I was thinking of having everything in muted avocado,' Audrey mused, examining a brochure. 'I'd like a ceramic hob, and a double oven. What's the matter?'

'We don't do muted avocado,' stammered the man. 'Then what's that?' said Audrey, showing him a colour chart in the brochure. He looked over her shoulder.

'That's a bathroom, ma'am.'

'Oh,' said Audrey, shuffling through her brochures, 'I was wondering what a carousel vegetable basket was doing in the bathroom cupboard.' She looked through another brochure and made an instant decision.

'I think I'll have Mandalay Teak – no, oak with infilled panels. Good British oak, "The Monarch of the Timbers",' she read out.

'May I recommend the German?' asked the kitchen fitter.

'Certainly not. I always buy British.'

'Most people . . .'

'I am not most people,' said Audrey emphatically. 'Honestly, I don't know how you persuade people to buy a "*Brotschrank*" and they don't even know what it is,' she went on, pointing to an item picked at random from a price list.

'It's a bread cupboard, ma'am. We're in Europe now, aren't we?'

'You may be, but I intend to stay here. As it happens, Europe appears to have come here,' she added, Richard DeVere never far from her mind.

'I'd also like a large worktop over here – over the fridge and the washing machine.'

They were joined by the man who had been measuring the bathroom, wanting to know whether Audrey had chosen her fittings.

'Oh, yes,' she said, leading him out into the hall. 'I rather like the look of the Nordic bath with the hydro air massage,' she improvized as she led him back upstairs.

Well, if you're going to have a fantasy, it might as well be a good one, she thought. Halfway up the stairs, she turned and looked back down to the sea of faces standing in the hall looking up at her.

'Who's Bedroom?' she enquired generally of the group.

One of the men owned up.

'Then come on up with me,' she commanded imperiously. 'You'd better get started, and I'll be with you just as soon as I've finished in the bathroom.'

'You'll need a carpet eight square metres exactly,' said Bathroom.

'Metres?' Audrey questioned. 'No, it just wouldn't fit. This house was built in feet and inches.'

If there was a misunderstanding going the rounds on the Grantleigh estate, the person who was bound to be behind it was the rector.

On this occasion he could be forgiven, for what is any sane man with neither guile nor malice to make of the sight of all those tradesmen's vans outside the lodge? Trades' descriptions on the sides of the vehicles led one to understand that certain structural or decorative services were being touted. It was a reasonable assumption that the owner of the house, outside which they were parked, was availing herself of them.

The rector was on the way to the manor on his bicycle, to rattle a collecting box at DeVere on behalf of blind ponies. The sight of all those vehicles gave him a news item which, in the manner of country parsons, would be shared with the next person he met – which happened to be DeVere.

'She must have come into some money,' said DeVere, sensing that the alterations suggested by the rector's report had to be paid for.

'I do hope so,' said the rector, rattling his collecting box by way of a hint which evinced a willing fiver from DeVere.

This transaction was conducted in the tea-room where DeVere had been closeting himself of late to catalogue the items in his china collection on both the advice of Constable Peaslake and an insurance company. It took more than a visit from the rector to make him stop work, and he continued the examination and listing of his pieces.

'I've never been in here before,' said the rector taking in his elegant surroundings.

'Not even in the fforbes-Hamiltons' time?'

'I don't think they had very much china.'

'No, they kept dropping it apparently.' DeVere held up a saucer.

'What would you say this was?'

'A saucer,' ventured the cleric.

'I know it's a saucer,' said an irritated DeVere. 'But is it a Staffordshire or a Dresden copy?'

'I wouldn't know. Mrs fforbes-Hamilton would know, though.'

The rector's remark was enough to remind DeVere that he had, in fact, been wasting his time. This was not a job for him – it was certainly one for Audrey.

He suggested that cataloguing the collection might be just

up Audrey's street.

'But she's frightfully busy at the moment,' said the rector.

'Ah, of course she is,' agreed DeVere, reminded of what was going on at the lodge.

It was not until this moment that DeVere appreciated the significance of the rector's revelations. Audrey had struck rich – that was what the evidence pointed to.

The thought that she might have come into some money by virtue of an Egyptian vase crossed his mind, but the thought perished. But it kept coming back. Was not Audrey about the only person who knew it was there? She knew what it was worth, she had access to the manor, she knew how to dispose of it, and, above all, she was spending money which she constantly purported to be short of. That was the tell-tale sign which Constable Peaslake had led him to keep an eye open for. DeVere tried to disassociate the two events, but the more he thought about it, it became increasingly obvious that Audrey qualified for all the policeman's criteria. Maybe the rector had been mistaken and there was some simpler explanation.

Yet the subject had to be broached and a painless way of doing so occurred to him. He went to the phone and dialled.

'It's Richard,' DeVere announced as he listened attentively to the background noises which could be heard down the line from the lodge.

'Have you got anybody with you, Audrey?'

'Of course not,' said Audrey. 'There aren't any workmen here.'

So why did she mention them at all?

'What can I do for you, Richard?'

'It's my china collection. I've got to catalogue it so that it can be properly insured. I need your expertise.'

'That's very flattering, Richard. I shall enjoy that enormously.'

'Can you come over now?'

'As soon as you like.'

'Meet me in the tea-room then,' said DeVere, setting Audrey aglow. He made the assignation sound straight out of a film romance which cast her as the heroine. She put the phone down and turned to confront the bevy of workmen who had stopped work to iisten to her conversation. Invited into the company of Richard DeVere, she had no further need of her charade and its principal actors could now be dismissed.

'I have decided that all your estimates are far too high,' she announced to nobody in particular. 'I'll get a little man from Harrods who can come and do the lot. Thank you very much for coming.'

With that, she bid them good-day, took her Burberry down from the coat peg in the hall, and was out of the house and on her way to the manor.

DeVere did not expect her so soon. She didn't give him much time to work out how the subject of burglary was to be introduced. Of course, the whole matter could be cleared up if he could find out where she got the money from for all her home improvements, and that was as far as he had thought, when she arrived. She pitched straight into the job in hand, identifying each piece of china with an expert eye as if she'd been doing it all her life. DeVere found himself impressed, and the opportunity to bring up what was on his mind receded fast.

It was not until the job was done and the catalogue almost complete, that he saw his chance.

'I haven't had so much fun for a long time,' Audrey said cheerily.

'I'm very grateful. I couldn't have done without you, you know.'

'I'm so delighted to find all these things in here. When you moved here, I thought you'd fill the place with gonks, Spanish dolls and ballerina cigarette lighters.'

'It's refreshing to find somebody who knows what's what. You should turn professional, you know.'

'I couldn't possibly afford to start.'

DeVere found himself edging towards the matter in his mind.

'One lucky find – that's all it takes,' he hinted. It evinced no positive reaction from Audrey.

'Think of the money,' he went on. It did get a reaction, but not the one he'd hoped for.

'There are a few of us left who don't do things just for money,' she said piously.

'But if you *had* the money, think what you could do. You could have all sorts of alterations done to the lodge – you could afford double glazing, new kitchen units, new bathroom,' he said pointedly, scrutinizing her for a look or a guilty twitch with every item. In fact, he felt he had been a bit unsubtle, but Audrey did not appear to grasp the implications.

'I'd much rather spend money on things like this,' she said, 'but as it is, I've just sold my last piece.'

DeVere was horror struck by the thought which now entered his head. She *had* sold it.

'Richard, isn't there something missing?' she asked, seemingly apropos of nothing, at least of nothing which was in her mind.

'Yes, there is. I give you three guesses.'

'The Egyptian vase.'

'I said three.'

'Where is it?'

'You don't know?'

'No.'

'It's been stolen.'

'How dreadful. Who on earth would steal it?'

DeVere saw his chance.

'I thought you might have some idea.'

'Why me?'

'Because you know the house so well.'

'I don't see how that helps.'

DeVere went into his prepared statement.

'Well,' he said, 'whoever stole it new firstly what they were looking for, secondly what it was worth, thirdly where to find it and fourthly how to get to it, and fifthly . . .'

Audrey butted in. 'But Richard, if you follow that line of reasoning, well, *I* could have done it.'

It was like a blow to the solar plexus.

'I suppose you could,' he said with feigned nonchalance after a silence. 'Mind you, it's a good job you're not spending a lot of money all of a sudden.'

'What's that got to do with it?'

'Oh, nothing, except the police said that all I have to do is wait for somebody local who appears to be spending more money than we know they have.'

'Well, there you are then. I haven't been spending money – not that I wouldn't have done if I had any.'

'Of course you would – on new kitchen units, double glazing, carpets, curtains, roof insulation and hundreds of other things that you say that you're not having done at the lodge.'

Audrey covered her obvious embarrassment with an outburst of laughter.

'I see, I see,' she said, when her guffaws had subsided. 'So you've been spying on me? Well, there is a perfectly rational explanation.' She reflected for a moment. 'Well, not that rational, I suppose. But true, anyway.'

DeVere remained silent to embarrass her into some explanation of her activities which she had at least now confessed.

'The truth is,' she sighed, 'that while Marjory and Brabinger have been away, I've been a bit lonely.'

This told him everything, but her attitude was not one of humility or penitence, or even as one explaining away irrational conduct – but as one whose actions were perfectly sane and rational. DeVere found himself being completely drawn into her logic.

'Then what was the piece you sold?' he asked to complete the missing element in the mystery.

'My Indian Buddha. Why?'

DeVere didn't answer, but sat at the table drubbing his fingers on the marquetry. It was enough for Audrey to twig what was in his mind. The accusations were now going the other way. She got up from the table and drew herself up to her full height.

'Richard,' she said sternly, 'surely you don't think . . .' But she was now convinced that he did. 'You thought it was your Egyptian vase?'

'No, never crossed my mind,' he said with feigned indifference.

'That's why you asked me over here – to accuse me.'

'I haven't accused you of anything.'

'You've dropped some very broad hints,' screamed Audrey, and repeated the foregoing conversation almost word for word to prove it.

The tirade was interrupted by the arrival of Mrs Polouvička and Marjory. Their entrance at that moment was unremarkable, except for the fact that Mrs Polouvička was cradling the subject of their conversation – £40,000 worth of ancient Egyptian vase.

'Where did you find that?' demanded DeVere, whose voice had already reached the enraged pitch set by Audrey's.

'This? We lent it to Marjory.'

Marjory substantiated the explanation.

'Yes, I'm so grateful, Mrs Poo.'

DeVere rushed at his mother and snatched the vase and held it lovingly to his chest.

Mutual greetings and welcomes seemed strangely out of place at this point, yet they were exchanged until DeVere could stand it no longer.

'Never mind the social chit-chat. What was Marjory doing with my Egyptian vase?' he demanded, sulkily.

Mrs Polouvička spoke up.

'She asked if we had any old jugs she could use in her play.'

It was Audrey who questioned the description.

'Old jugs!?'

'You told me it was old yourself,' said Mrs Poo.

'You've got no idea how perfect it was,' enthused Marjory innocently. 'Cleopatra kept her asp in it. It was simply superb,' she said. It became clear that Marjory's drama course had taught her something about histrionics, and the account was related with the full dramatic effect with voice and gesture.

'Imagine the effect,' she declaimed in hushed tones. 'Everybody on stage is dead . . . and the only movement on the stage . . . is the vase . . . rolling around and then down to the front of the stage . . . rumble, rumble . . . and off into the pit.'

'Oh, my God,' groaned its owner. 'This is a precious antique.'

'How could it be? It was chipped,' scorned his mother. Audrey came to judgement.

'Marjory, do you realize what you've done? Richard's been out of his mind with worry.'

'I said she could have it,' said the old woman, almost daring anyone to gainsay her right to do so. But Marjory was duly humbled.

'If I'd known what it was, I would never have let Cleopatra hurl it at the third eunuch,' she assured them. DeVere whimpered, and hugged the vase closer to him. It seemed the end of the matter, and at least no harm was done.

'So, what's been going on while we've been away?' Marjory said, to relieve the tense atmosphere.

'I've been helping Richard catalogue his china collection,'

replied Audrey, to challenge the implied suggestion that they had been getting together for less honourable or less practical reasons.

'Oh, good. So you haven't been lonely then?'

The word 'lonely' struck chords of bitter memory in Mrs Polouvička's mind.

'Lonely?' she asked. 'Who's lonely?'

'Audrey thought she might be while I was away.'

'Oh, you need never be lonely,' the old lady assured her. 'If ever you get lonely, do what I used to do.'

DeVere asked what that was.

'Well, when you were on business, I used to get all the tradesmen round to measure the place for free estimates – carpets, curtains, kitchen floors, double glazing – the lot. Never bought anything, but I did it just for the company.'

It was the first DeVere had heard of it.

'You never said anything to me, mother.'

'Of course not. You would have thought I'd gone quite ga-ga.'

This amused DeVere.

'Yes,' he agreed. 'I would have thought that, wouldn't you, Marjory?'

'Gosh, yes. Quite ga-ga,' she chuckled.

'Completely off your head.'

They all laughed, with the exception of Audrey, whom DeVere was gentleman enough to bring back into the conversation. She had gone strangely quiet.

'Now, you would never do a thing like that, would you, Audrey?'

'No,' Audrey lied, and tried to smile.

5

To be thought capable of theft, to be so grossly misjudged and wronged, was not without its advantages. Audrey was the injured party in their relationship, and that meant Richard DeVere owed her a favour. DeVere knew it, and spent many soul-searching hours wondering how to redeem himself. Audrey knew that he knew, and decided to let him stew. She did not make contact with him for several weeks, knowing that some excuse to resume communication would turn up in due course without it appearing to be at her instigation. In short, she gave him the kind of cold-shouldering treatment which in matters of the heart drives a man into the arms of another woman. This possibility did not occur to her until it was almost too late.

It all started the day Richard DeVere had his first fall from a horse. It was an occasion Audrey remembered more particularly as the day the lodge began falling about her ears. The previous night there had been a violent storm even by the harsh standards of the Grantleigh Valley which was a perpetual wind-trap. Audrey awoke that morning to find water gushing in through the spare room roof, and a heap of broken tiles pitting the front flower bed.

Sending Ned on to the roof to inspect the damage was not a wise move, as it happened, in view of what she would have seen by doing the job herself. If she had been up on the roof, she would have had a grandstand view of Richard DeVere, huntsman, coming a cropper. But at least she was in the front line to witness the humiliation of his return home as he limped past the lodge leading his horse.

'Oh, poor Richard. Did you fall?' she said as if she had not already had the benefit of a detailed account of the catastrophe from Ned.

'Horse tripped over one of those damned dogs,' sighed DeVere, very disgruntled.

'Hounds, not dogs,' she corrected. 'No bones broken, I hope,' she said, advancing towards him as if to feel him over.

'I'm a bit sore, but . . .'

Audrey had passed him by on her way to the horse, giving its limbs the once-over that DeVere had been expecting for himself. She satisfied herself that the beast was still sound.

'And what about . . .?'

'The hedge?' interruped DeVere. 'Oh, no, that's not broken either. Went clean over the top.'

'No. You.'

'Oh, me?' said DeVere, with apparent surprise that his well-being should even be this high in her priorities. 'Well, I must admit to being a bit shaken.'

'The ground comes up at you very fast, doesn't it?'

'And hard.'

'Well, you must get your confidence back. Now, get straight back on again,' she said imperiously, pointing at the saddle.

DeVere hesitated.

'Come along,' she ordered, with a no-nonsense manner. 'Up you get – into the saddle with you – and ride home.'

He let himself be persuaded and mounted clumsily.

'You let the horse know who's master – you or it,' said Audrey, giving the horse a hearty whack on the rump.

Horse and rider lurched off down the drive, apparently intent on parting company before long.

'*It*, I think,' Audrey judged, as she gazed after him and roared with laughter.

For all his shortcomings as a horseman, Audrey took the fact of DeVere's going hunting as an indication that he was beginning to settle down and take country life a bit more seriously. She welcomed it with relief, tarnished with nostalgia and regret for the end of her own hunting days. She could no longer afford it. And though he had frequently asked her to join him in the field, that meant him providing horse and hunt fees which would be accepting the dreaded charity.

It was a curious thing about Audrey's attitude in the matter of charity, that she had never once regarded her reduced circumstances as any obstacle to giving help or solace or whatever the importunate required. She may have grumbled quietly to herself or Marjory, but in the end she always delivered the goods. And so it was to be in the case of an old school friend, who, according to a letter which arrived the following day, appeared to be hurling herself at Audrey for help. The letter reported such a sequence of disasters that Audrey concluded that the poor girl had in the intervening years messed her life up completely.

'You remember Podge, don't you?' she said to Marjory, who had called round that day.

'Podge? Oh, Podge Hodge from school. Yes.'

'Well, she's coming to stay.'

'Here?'

'Where else? This weekend.'

Memories of Podge Hodge came flooding back. The school fatso who compensated for her excess bulk with entertainment value, and who had been much in demand throughout her school days to pad up and fill goal mouths for hockey matches and 'lacs' – lacrosse.

'Oh, it'll be marvellous to see her again,' Marjory exulted. 'Can't have seen her for twenty years.'

'Nor have I.'

'Podge Hodge, eh? Gosh, she was fun, wasn't she?'

'We should have a marvellous weekend,' said Marjory hopefully.

'I'm not sure,' said Audrey with a hint of caution, taking the letter from the mantelpiece and passing it over. 'It seems she's recovering from a rather unsavoury divorce.'

'I'm surprised she ever got married at all,' said Marjory. 'I mean, she wasn't exactly – er – pretty, was she?'

'Let's not mince words, Marjory. She had a face like a ship's boiler, and a figure like a pile of lifebelts.'

'Thought more of horses than she did of men.'

'Yes, she probably fed her husband bran mash and rubbed him down with a dandy brush before he went to work in the mornings.'

They both laughed. Audrey looked at the envelope that the letter had come in, and appeared to go off it very suddenly.

'It's addressed to the lodge,' she said in amazement. 'How did Podge know?'

Marjory swallowed guiltily.

'It's in the *Old Girls' Magazine*,' she said, unearthing the stapled mimeographed pamphlet from her basket.

'Mine came this morning,' she added, tossing it over.

Audrey looked at it suspiciously.

'What?' she yelled suddenly as she perused the offending sheet. 'This is for old girls' news, I grant you, but not for scandal.'

'Where's the scandal?'

Audrey flipped through the pages.

'There. My name is under "Change of Circumstances".' She read the relevant passage. "Audrey has left Grantleigh Manor" – spelt wrong – "and now lives down the drive." 'Honestly, Marjory,' she said indignantly, 'it makes it sound as if I live in a pothole. Where did they get all this information?'

'The area secretary sends it in.'

'And who is this area secretary?'

'I am.'

Audrey glared at her.

'Call yourself a friend.'

She looked at the magazine again.

'And you've put my phone number. So they'll all be telephoning me now to cluck and gloat, and in the summer they'll turn up in hordes to commiserate with me on their way to their holiday homes in Cornwall, and I'll be expected to give them lunch.'

'You used to like seeing old school friends.'

'At the manor, yes. There I could cope with their stockbroker husbands and their seventeen children spilling Ribena on the Wilton and blocking up all the lavatories. Really, Marjory, fancy letting a thing like this out.'

Marjory had little defence except to suggest that other old girls had much worse things written about them in the magazine.

'Such as?' Audrey demanded.

'Well, Wanda Fairbrother is down to sending her children to the local school.'

'Oh. Where do they live now?'

'Harrow.'

'I expect she'll turn up as well next week. Podge Hodge is just the thin end of the wedge, if you can describe her as the thin end of anything. It's bad enough her having to see me in this rabbit hutch.'

Audrey went over to the window and looked out at her beloved manor.

'Ironic, isn't it?' she said. 'There's DeVere in that house rattling around in twenty-four bedrooms, and me in this little two-up and two-down, inviting the whole world to stay.'

'Not the whole world, Audrey. Just Podge,' said Marjory, trying to bring her back to reality. 'She may be big, but she only needs one room.'

The mention of the one room needed by Podge reminded Audrey that she hadn't now got even that.

'Oh, my lord,' she groaned, 'I can't put her in there. It hasn't got a roof on it.

'Oh. Well, there's Brabinger's room.'

'He's an old man, Marjory. You can't throw him out.'

'Well, you'll have to put her off, then.'

'No,' said Audrey – a spirit of *noblesse oblige* coming to the fore, 'that would be dereliction of duty. Poor Podge is trying to rebuild a new life from the ruins of her past, and it's only natural she should want to see me. She's desperate, poor lamb.'

'She must be,' said Marjory.

A solution to this impasse was already floating around in Audrey's mind in the shape of Richard DeVere rattling around in his twenty-four bedrooms.

'No,' said Audrey suddenly turning cheerful. 'Richard will put her up.'

'Richard?'

'Why not? He owes me a favour and it's time we saw each other again.'

'But that would be handing him another woman on a plate.'

Audrey laughed.

'Podge? Don't be ridiculous. She'd flatten him. And break the plate. Besides, I do credit him with a bit of taste.'

Marjory could see her point.

Within seconds, the whole visit was settled. Podge would eat with them at the lodge, and sleep at the manor. And before long, Podge's whole programme was worked out. The only oversight was Richard DeVere's agreement to the plan, and Audrey was soon on her way to the manor to bring this tiresome and trifling detail to his attention.

If Audrey accepted that her hunting days were over – at

least for the present – DeVere did not. He had tried to get back into her good books by pestering her to go hunting, and didn't let the matter drop.

When she arrived at the manor, he raised the subject again.

'I think I need to go with someone experienced,' he admitted, and she had to agree.

'I can see that, but I'm afraid I've got this schoolfriend coming.'

'Well, you can bring her along,' he suggested, anxious to please.

Audrey's memory of Podge was that when she wasn't on the hockey field in a padded track suit, or red-legged in lacs togs, she was in jodhpurs lapping a gymkhana show ring. A good hunt was probably just what she needed this weekend. Her needs and DeVere's offer seemed to be made for each other.

'Podge would love that,' she said.

'Podge?'

'Podge Hodge. That's what we called her at school. But there is a problem.'

'I can imagine.'

'No, seriously. I've got a few tiles loose.'

'*You* said it!'

'You're not helping, Richard. I'm trying to ask you a favour. Could you find it in your heart to give Podge a bed for the weekend?'

'Be glad to. A double bed?'

'That should get her all in.'

Audrey explained the dilemma, and it was soon agreed that Podge would have the Chinese room for the weekend. Audrey noticed DeVere over-reacting to the prospect and rubbing his hands with glee which she felt was probably intended to get some jealous reaction from her.

'I must warn you, Richard, Podge is getting over a rather nasty divorce.'

‘A gay divorcee, eh? Sounds promising.’

‘Furthermore, she’s no oil painting, and if she’s hunting with you, you’ll have to find her a very large horse.’

Her account of Podge seemed to do little to dampen DeVere’s interest in this creature. It never actually occurred to him that Audrey was merely outlining the facts of the case. He put Audrey’s description of her down to female cattiness.

When the weekend came, DeVere insisted on being at the lodge to witness her arrival. While they waited, Marjory showed DeVere the old school photograph, pointing out herself, then Audrey and Podge, who, even then, presented such a terrifying aspect that the sight of just her picture sent a gulp of sherry down the wrong way.

‘Heaven help us,’ spluttered DeVere.

‘She was always anchor man in our house tug-of-war team,’ said Marjory, matter-of-factly.

‘Poor Viscount,’ DeVere sympathized, explaining, ‘That’s the horse she’s riding tomorrow.’

Audrey came into the room bearing an old army kit bag, containing her late husband’s hunting clothes, which Brabinger had extracted from the attic. Audrey rummaged in the dusty kit bag and brought out a pair of wide-girthed jodhpurs.

‘Yes, I think she should get into these.’

She was just on the way to get Brabinger to press them when the doorbell rang. She put the jodhpurs back in the kit bag and hid it behind the sofa. Marjory made for the door.

‘Brabinger will answer it, Marjory,’ said Audrey disporting herself just inside the door to receive her guest.

‘Yes, he’ll squeeze her in somehow,’ agreed DeVere laughing.

Audrey rounded on him.

‘That’ll do, Richard. I shall expect you to treat her like any normal human being. We’ve got to try and bring her out – rehabilitate her and bring her confidence back.

'I get the picture,' said DeVere. 'It's like getting back on a horse.'

'Exactly.'

The door opened and Brabinger announced 'Miss Hodge, Madam.'

No sooner had he spoken than he was almost bowled over in the slipstream of Podge's perfumed and bejewelled entrance, and was buried beneath her discarded fur coat.

'Darlings,' gushed a slim, poised and beautiful creature as she swept into the room, barely recognized by the welcoming party. Gone was the *en bon point*, and the puppy fat of yesteryear. Threaded down the middle of it all that time must have been this sylphlike beauty who, at some point in the last twenty years, had shed that adolescent cocoon of adipose tissue.

Audrey and Marjory were speechless, and while they adjusted their perceptive organs to the new scale, Podge continued to regale them.

'How lovely to see you. Why, you haven't changed a bit – either of you.'

'Thank you,' said Audrey, still suffering shock. 'Nor have you,' she lied.

'Well, this is going to be fun, isn't it?' said the vision in her slinky blue dress with the split halfway up the leg. 'All the old girls together.'

'Not quite,' said DeVere stepping out of the shadows.

Audrey had forgotten about him, and introduced him. As they sniffed out each other's credentials, as dogs do but not in that precise manner, Audrey was whispering to Marjory.

'I don't believe it,' she said. 'How do you get from WXXX down to that?'

'And so pretty,' added Marjory enviously.

This put a completely different complexion on things. How could this woman, who even now seemed to be engulfing Richard DeVere be sent to the manor to sleep with him? Dare they put temptation in his way? Another solution to the accommodation problem had to be found. But she only got as far as suggesting that Podge went to an hotel on account of the leaking roof, when DeVere intervened to remind her that arrangements had already been made.

'She's sleeping in the Chinese room, remember?'

'She can't possibly,' Audrey objected. 'It's the monsoon season,' as if that was a satisfactory deterrent.

There was nothing she could do to change the plan while DeVere was so obviously holding her to it, and was so obviously aglow at the prospect of this woman's company for the night, and indeed for the following day, too. Had not the hunting also become a fixed point in the weekend?

'I'm lending you a horse,' he promised.

'She couldn't possibly,' protested Audrey. 'We haven't got any clothes that would fit her. I mean, Marton's are far too big.'

'Why can't she borrow yours?' said DeVere. 'You must be the same size.'

It was no good protesting. The more obstacles she put in the way, the more DeVere reminded her that everything was her idea in the first place. She tried to hustle him out of the house before the instant shine which he had so obviously taken to Podge became a positive blaze of passion. He eventually took the hint and got up.

'Well, come over when you're ready, Miss Hodge. I usually have an early night before a hunt. I'll call you in plenty of time. Tea or coffee?'

'Tea, please,' said Podgc.

'China, Indian, Ceylon, Lapsang Suchong?'

'Well, if it's in the Chinese room, it had better be China.'

'Milk?'

'Please.'

'Cow's, goat's, camel's?'

Audrey brought him to heel with a stern 'Richard!' and

turned to Podge. 'You must forgive him – he only speaks in lists – he's a grocer.'

With that, she had Brabinger see him out of the house.

'What an absolutely smashing man,' gasped Podge when he had gone.

'Brabinger? Yes, he's a boon.'

'No – Richard.'

Audrey turned solemn for a moment and allowed herself a pause while she thought hard and fast.

'I think I must warn you about him, Podge. He's not quite himself at the moment.'

She and Marjory began to regale Podge with a duet of foreboding on the matter of Richard DeVere.

'He hasn't got over the loss of his wife yet.'

'He's extremely demoralized and leans on us a good deal.'

'Yes, we look after him.'

'Eventually we hope to rehabilitate him completely, but at the moment he mustn't be upset in any way at all.'

Podge seemed to have her own thoughts on the subject.

'But aren't you lucky,' she said. 'I mean, having a man like that on your doorstep. You could do a lot worse for yourself, Audrey. Still, I don't suppose the gay divorcee can tell the merry widow anything she doesn't already know.'

The soubriquet did not fit Audrey's self-image.

'I'm not exactly a merry widow.'

Marjory substantiated the point with 'Poor Audrey. She misses the manor dreadfully.'

'I'm so sorry,' said Podge. 'It must have been very distressing.'

'Oh, it was,' Audrey agreed. 'And at such an inconvenient time, too. I'd just had a new lot of writing paper printed.'

Marjory tried to change the subject before Audrey got morose.

'What rotten luck about your divorce, Podge,' she said, hardly improving things.

'On the contrary,' Podge replied. 'Booting the old man out like that was the best thing I ever did. Now I'm footloose and fancy free for the first time in my life.'

The two girls were horrified at the thought that this vamp and they could possibly be the product of the same school.

A silence fell on the room which reminded Podge of another absentee.

'Oh, I forgot,' she said, springing up. 'Can I bring Twinkle in?'

'Twinkle?'

'My dog. She's no trouble. You don't mind dogs, do you?'

'Oh, no, we love them.'

As she left the room, Audrey and Marjory were galvanized into a flurry of conversation as they exchanged ideas for the solution to their quandary.

'We've got to put a stop to this.'

'I know. Did you see the looks she and Richard were giving each other?'

'We cannot allow them to be alone together at the manor.'

'I did warn you.'

'Well, tell her there's been a frightful mistake – we forgot that there's a full moon tonight, and DeVere is liable to go off his head. So we'll put her in Brabinger's room for safety.'

'With Brabinger?'

'No, no. Of course not. Brabinger will have to sleep on the sofa.'

'But I thought you said we can't ask an old man to get out of his room.'

'Never mind what I said. This is an emergency. Brabinger will sleep on the sofa.'

Their parley was interrupted by the reappearance of Podge, who swept in carrying a hairy tartan rug which she threw over the sofa. She was followed by a huge great dane who almost filled the entire doorway.

'Come on, Twinkle,' she called, and the brute padded its slobbery way into the room.

Bertie growled and ran outside. Audrey growled but stayed.

'This is Twinkle, everybody. She'll be no trouble. Shc can sleep on the sofa.' With that, the animal leapt on to the sofa where, with the exception of the occasional meal time, it stayed for the entire weekend.

Dawn broke over Grantleigh manor the following morning. It usually did. DeVere woke up and remembered that he had a desirable female staying in the house. He leapt out of bed, bathed, shaved, dowsed himself in all manner of talcs, and after-shave lotions, groomed himself and then put on a clean pair of pyjamas and a robe to give the impression that he had just woken up and that this was the worst he was ever likely to look.

He went downstairs, remembering his guest's order from the night before, and made tea – China tea. He then made his way back upstairs bearing a tray, hovered a moment to make last-minute adjustments to his grooming outside the door of the Chinese room, and knocked diffidently.

There was no reply. He had hoped there would not be. He opened the door and crept into the darkened room. He put down the tray on the bedside table and drew the curtains.

'Room Service. China tea as ordered. It's seven o'clock, Miss Hodge. Wakey, wakey, rise and shine.'

The mound in the Chinese bed, enveloped by a gold-thread dragon, did not stir.

'Lovely hunting weather. Beautiful, crisp morning,' DeVere sang out. The heap of bedclothes did not stir.

'Miss Hodge? Time to get up.' The best way to get a reaction seemed to be by physical contact. This was exactly what DeVere had hoped. He looked at the shape underneath the bedclothes and made a grasp for what he took to be a shoulder and shook it gently.

The body wriggled and a head emerged from the bedding. It was Brabinger's.

Brabinger read the look of abject horror on DeVere's face as being no more than that of mild surprise.

'I'm sorry about this, sir. Mrs fforbes-Hamilton sent me over – she's sub-let my room.'

DeVere was considerably relieved to find that Brabinger was not going to be his hunting companion for the day as well.

Podge turned up at the stable at a suitable hour and made her acquaintance with Viscount. Since the meet was at the manor, they did not have to allow time to get to the hunt, which meant that they had plenty of time to get to know each other.

'I'm sorry about last night,' said Podge. 'Only we drank an awful lot of Brabinger's homemade wine, and I was out for the count. Terribly rude of me,' she apologized.

'Well, I got the fright of my life when I woke you up this morning,' said DeVere.

'I can imagine.'

By the time the hunt set off from the meet in the manor forecourt, DeVere and Podge Hodge were getting on famously, and indeed they were on first name terms. The name 'Podge' had been dropped from DeVere's considerations altogether – and the name Diana was substituted. This was the name that Audrey heard DeVere using as the two of them trailed at the end of the line of horses as the hunt passed the lodge. Audrey's ears did not deceive her when she heard them laughing riotously at what seemed to be some intimate, private joke. Nor did her eyes, aided and abetted by her binoculars when she saw the two of them behaving as if in a world of their own, and oblivious of the rest of the hunt. Ever since releasing her old schoolfriend to

DeVere's charge for the day's activities – to honour an agreement – Audrey had been keeping an eye on them. She did not intend to stop now, just because they were moving out of range and on horseback.

At the sight of Podge and DeVere together, something seized her – its name was jealousy.

'Where's your bicycle?' demanded Audrey, lowering her binoculars as DeVere and Podge had turned into a field just out of range of the lodge.

'Outside. Why?' asked Marjory.

Audrey threw down the binoculars, ran out into the hall, grabbed her coat and jumped on to Marjory's bicycle. By the time she had joined the bevy of foot-followers, she had lost sight of the field – at least, it was too far away for her to be able to identify individual riders and horses. She had to rely for her information on a running commentary being provided by Ned who was following the action through a pair of binoculars. As usual he had chosen a good vantage point from which to view the proceedings – the lodge roof.

'There goes Charlie Fox, heading for Ashcombe covet. The pack's gaining on him though. Hasn't got a chance if he goes to ground in there. There goes the master, going round the other side. Ha. Charlie's beaten him to it. He's out the other side – good old Charlie – he's losing them.'

'Who's leading the field, Ned?' asked Audrey. She yelled from her bicycle which was ready to take any road which led to the action.

'The brigadier, Mrs fforbes-Hamilton. The rest is in a bunch, except for two falling behind at the back.'

Audrey looked suspicious.

'Well, where are they off to?'

Ned continued. 'They're going into Little Spinney. They must be after something.'

'That's very possible,' said Audrey, not doubting for a moment in her suspicious mind who the two stragglers might be.

Ned continued his commentary.

'Well, if my sight's anything to go by, I'd say that was Mr DeVere and . . .'

As the foot-followers once more took to their vehicles and headed in one direction, Audrey made off in the other. As far as she was concerned, the action was still in Little Spinney, which was where the two back markers had gone astray and were probably up to no good. She took the nearest road route to Little Spinney.

The road only took her part of the way, and in turning into a field to take the 'as the crow flies' route to her objective, Audrey had forgotten that she was not a crow. She hurtled straight into a ploughed field. The bicycle stopped, but her momentum had other ideas. She flew over the handle bars and landed on her face in a pool of mud. For her, the day's hunt was over.

For all the good it did Audrey to come home, have a bath, clean up, and sit in the warm for a while with a stiff drink, she might as well have lain in the mud all afternoon. Neither were her spirits any the brighter by the time evening fell, nor after two hours of darkness, by which time DeVere and Podge had not returned from the hunting field.

'They're up to no good, mark my words,' she snapped to Marjory, who had been invited to dinner. 'It's sex, that's what it is.'

'Not in the dark, surely?' offered Marjory.

'The darkness is no obstacle. The cold might be a bit inhibiting, I agree.'

It was then that Marjory hit on the truth, and Audrey resented it.

'You don't like the competition, do you?'

'That's not the point. It's our duty to save Richard from making a terrible mistake. Podge is not the girl we used to know.'

Marjory conceded that much.

Audrey went on.

'You heard what she said – footloose and fancy free – well, we don't want somebody like that at the manor, do we?'

There was no doubt that Audrey had been considering the long-term prospects of this present little intrigue.

At that moment, the doorbell rang and Marjory leapt up.

'Don't get so excited, Marjory. A chilly reception is what they deserve, and that's what they're going to get.'

They positioned themselves just inside the door and closed ranks to maximize the effect of the chilly reception.

The door opened.

'Here we are, Audrey,' sang DeVere casually. 'One old schoolfriend delivered safe and sound.'

'I'm glad to hear it,' said Audrey with anything but gladness in her voice.

'Gosh, I'm exhausted,' said Podge.

'Good hunting, was it?' asked Audrey.

Podge seemed to pick up the implication.

'I was teaching him a few tricks,' she said. 'He's a quick learner, I'll say that. I think I'd better get changed.'

'Yes, you'd better,' said Audrey archly. 'Dinner won't be long. In fact, it was half an hour ago.'

'I'm awfully sorry – you shouldn't have waited. We had something in the pub.'

Podge Hodge yawned.

'Oh dear, I feel like crawling into bed right now.'

'Feel free,' said DeVere hopefully, but Audrey would hear none of it.

'Marjory, you take Podge upstairs and deal with my wet clothes.'

Marjory and Podge went upstairs, leaving DeVere to face the music. He had no idea what was coming to him and relaxed into the sofa, or as much of it as was not occupied by one great dane named Twinkle.

'Move up, you lazy hound,' he said, slapping the beast on the backside.

'That's a dog, not a hound,' corrected Audrey. 'Now, why are you so late?'

'We were enjoying ourselves.'

'I was afraid you might be.'

'That was supposed to be the general idea, wasn't it? I was only doing it for you. She cheered up a lot, you know.'

'She doesn't want cheering up.'

'But you told me she did.'

'It's all been a dreadful mistake. I didn't know, you see.'

'Know what?'

'Well, I can scarcely bring myself to say it about a fellow old girl, but Podge is a fallen woman. She's only out for what she can get, and she's eaten bigger men than you for breakfast.'

'She didn't get the chance this morning. You saw to that.'

'I was trying to protect you, Richard. You see, you're playing with fire. She'll play it fast and loose with you, grab what she can while the going's good, and then she'll be off.'

'Well, she's going tomorrow, anyway.'

'But there's always tonight.'

DeVere realized the nature of her concern.

'Oh, so that's what's been bothering you. Well, you don't have to worry. I mean, we're getting on pretty well, but there's nothing like *that*, I assure you.'

Wonderful the innuendo you can get into a word like 'that'.

'I wish I could be certain,' said Audrey.

'You have my word as a gentleman and a grocer.'

Marjory came down to report that while she had been able to bring down Podge's wet hunting clothes, she had been unable to do the same with Podge herself, who had slumped down on Audrey's bed and was now asleep.

'Then let her sleep,' said Audrey. 'At least then she can't get up to mischief.'

'I must say I could do with a bit of shut-eye too,' said DeVere, getting up and showing his eagerness to get back to the manor. 'Oh, do me a favour, Audrey,' he said as an afterthought. 'Don't send Brabinger over to sleep at the manor again. He gave me the fright of my life.'

Audrey kept her promise. The following morning when DeVere opened the door of the Chinese room, bearing his tray, he was relieved to find a lady's vanity case and toilet requisites, as he knew them to be called in the supermarket business, on the dressing table and a lady's dressing gown draped over the chair beside the bed.

'Good morning, Diana,' he said. He put down the tray and went over to the curtains and drew them. 'Lovely day again. No hunting today, but I expect we can find something to do. Mind you, you don't have to go, you know. You can stay a bit longer if you like.'

The mound in the bed did not stir.

Surer of his ground this time, DeVere went closer to the bed and grabbed what he thought to be a shoulder and jiggled it. There was no reaction. He pulled back the bedclothes slightly to reveal a damp riding cap sitting on the pillow. He pulled the blankets further back to reveal not the voluptuous body he had anticipated, but an old army kit bag full of outsized hunting clothes.

'Diana,' he said as if the haberdashery before him was what she had been transformed into overnight.

The door slammed behind him. Propelling it was Audrey's foot. Audrey was fully dressed and gave the impression of having been up a considerable time, in preparation for this moment of truth.

'Caught you,' she sang. 'Good morning, Richard,' she said innocently.

She noticed two cups on the tray by the bedside.

'Oh, is that my tea?' she said. 'How kind. It's quite like old times to be sleeping at the manor again.'

She poured a cup and handed it to the speechless DeVere.

'Won't you join me?' she said.

'Um,' said DeVere.

6

Nothing brings people out into the fresh air quite like the first spell of freak sunshine towards the end of winter. Should this 'false spring' fall at a weekend, one will see every bridlepath and footpath being trodden by dedicated up-early ramblers, booted and rucksacked, striding purposefully across the countryside. Occasionally you will see them stop and get their bearings by consulting, more likely than not, *Somerset Walks* – that invaluable series of little guide books by W. H. Hartop, the county historian and tireless walker.

But for those less keen on fresh air and exercise, there is another reason for taking to the highways and byways on foot. That is when finding oneself without that vital adjunct to remote, rural life – the motor car.

Audrey fforbes-Hamilton was in the latter category.

'Where's the Rolls?' asked Marjory as she and Audrey passed the empty lodge garage on their way back from church that first glorious Sunday in March.

'It's gone in,' sighed Audrey sadly.

'About time.'

'Yes, but I'm afraid this time I won't be able to afford to get it out again,' she said wistfully. 'It'll be ages before I can pay the bill.'

'Don't worry,' comforted Marjory. 'There are lots of people on the estate who can give you lifts everywhere.'

'That's accepting charity. I can't do that. I mean, can you

see me taking lifts in Ned's tractor or in Miller's Land-Rover with a dead cow in the back?'

'No, but I bet if Richard DeVere came by in his Rolls and offered you a lift, you'd accept like a shot.'

'Would I just?' Audrey snapped. 'Anyway, we're not speaking at the moment.'

(Nor had they since the Podge Hodge incident.)

'I'm not surprised.'

'What do you mean?'

'Well, every time you do speak to him these days, you're always tearing him apart about something or arguing or trying to humiliate him. You two only ever meet up to have a battle these days.'

'So?'

'Well, if you met him casually from time to time and just passed the time of day together, I'm sure you two would get on a lot better.'

'You mean like in his car if he gave me a lift?'

'Exactly. Mind you, I don't know why I'm giving you this good advice.'

'Because, Marjory, you're my only friend and ally these days. Are you coming in for coffee?'

'Yes. But I'd much rather be driving through the country lanes with Richard DeVere. Imagine him whisking you off into the countryside, running out of petrol in the moonlight. Then he leans over towards you and whispers – "Alone at last . . .!"'

'Oh, do stop, Marjory. That sort of thing only happens in cartoons.'

Their conversation was abruptly ended by a spectacle which confronted them when they got to the lodge.

A crocodile of about twenty people was marching through the garden in a long line reaching up to the house. In fact, two middle-aged women in windcheaters and bobble hats, each shouldering a rucksack and carrying the Hartop guide, were actually staring in at the kitchen window.

'What a darling little house,' gushed one.

'It must be wonderful to live in the country,' enthused the other. 'I wonder if anybody actually lives here?'

'Yes, I think somebody must – there's dirty dishes on the sink.'

'Fancy. And at this time on a Sunday.'

Audrey and Marjory looked at each other in horror.

'What on earth do they think they're doing?' exclaimed Audrey, stepping up the pace to confront the intruders.

'Excuse me,' said Audrey challenging one of the women. 'May I ask what you're up to?'

The woman looked at her affronted.

'Oh, and who are you when you're at home?'

'I'm Mrs fforbes-Hamilton, and I *am* at home. Do you realize that this is private property?'

'Is it?' said the other lady innocently. 'Well, you'd better see Mr Hartop about that.' She indicated an elderly man with a weatherbeaten face and a wisp of white hair on one side of his head which, blown by the wind, left the other side of his head completely bald. He was at the head of the column, which had reached the garden gate. Audrey recognized him both as a visiting speaker to the WI, and as some functionary she'd seen at his job at the county town library.

'This woman wants a word with you,' called one of the ramblers.

The said Mr Hartop turned and came back towards the lodge.

'Can I help you?' he asked innocently.

'Certainly you can,' bellowed Audrey. 'What do you mean by tramping through my garden?'

'Oh, I beg your pardon. Is this your garden?' he said, looking at the weeds and the overgrown vegetation.

'Of course it is. What do you think it is – a public right of way?'

'Well, actually, yes,' said Mr Hartop.

'What in heaven's name are you talking about?' Audrey barked.

'This,' he said, pointing to the path which ran along the edge of the garden and out through the gate in the bottom hedge. 'This is a public right of way. It's the old Pilgrims' Way. In the old days the monks used to take this path. It leads to Glastonbury.'

'It leads to my compost heap, thank you very much.'

'The monks used it in the Middle Ages,' the old man went on.

'And what would they, or you, be wanting with my compost heap?'

'To get to Glastonbury to worship at the shrine where Joseph of Arimathaea is said to have buried the chalice that was used at the Last Supper. It's all in here,' he said, brandishing a copy of Hartop's *Somerset Walks*.

'Oh, how fascinating,' Marjory interjected.

'Quiet, Marjory,' ordered Audrey and turned to Mr Hartop. 'Yes, I know all about the Glastonbury legend, but are you telling me that anyone can tramp over my land?'

'Apparently so,' explained Mr Hartop. 'This is the latest edition of the guide, just published. It's the first one in which we have a complete account of the route the pilgrims used to take. Look,' he said, unfolding a map of the county from the centre pages of the booklet.

Audrey examined it and flicked through the pages.

'Who wrote this nonsense?'

'I did,' admitted Hartop.

'How dare you? Who are you to decide that all and sundry can tramp through my garden?'

'It's not me. This is an historic right of way. It's listed as protected.'

'And so it is. By me.'

'But surely you knew?'

'It's the first I've heard of it.'

'But when I researched this book I had the full cooperation of the owner of the Grantleigh Estate.'

'Really? You mean Mr DeVere?'

'Yes, I spoke to him about it last year.'

'He said nothing to me,' said Audrey angrily. She stamped her foot. 'Right.'

Audrey turned and stormed off in the direction of the manor.

'What about our cup of coffee?' Marjory called after her.

'It can wait,' Audrey replied. 'I think it's time I had another meeting with Mr DeVere.'

'Then don't forget what I said,' Marjory shouted. 'Make it casual.'

DeVere was enjoying his Sunday, blissfully unaware that in a few moments it would be in ruins. He was firmly convinced that winter was over, the sunshine apparently symbolizing a welcome breathing space at the end of a hard week of negotiations concluding in a satisfactory deal which left his mind and his timetable freer to consider more personal things. He was spending a rare quiet day with his mother. While he had many interests and concerns which craved his attention in such moments, his mother had just one – Audrey.

'I've got it,' said Mrs Polouvička.

'Then don't give it to me,' mumbled DeVere over his newspaper.

'Don't be cheeky, child. I'm talking about Audrey.'

'Hi-ho,' sighed DeVere.

'I have discovered what's wrong between you two.'

'And what would that be?'

'You're never alone together.'

'I'm alone with her quite a lot.'

'Ah, but not *alone* alone. You only ever meet up to have an argument or a squabble about something. She only comes here and you only go over there when you two have something to fight about – or if you want something. You never seem to meet up just casually and just pass the time of day together.'

'Well, she goes her way and I go mine. It's just that our paths don't cross very much.'

'And that is exactly what is wrong, my boy. You should bump into her by chance in the town more often.'

'That situation never arises, does it? I can't help that.'

'Yes, you can,' insisted the old lady. 'There are such things as chance meetings, but they have to be arranged,' she said with implicit wisdom. 'I happen to know that she is without her car at the moment. She would like to be offered a lift perhaps.'

He secretly liked the idea but did not dare show it.

'Fine, if I happen to be passing.'

'You *will* be passing,' screamed the old lady. She had it all worked out. 'Now, she goes shopping on Friday mornings. She'll be walking along the Marlbury Road.'

'That happens to be the very day my car is going in for a service, too – so that rules that out, doesn't it?'

Mrs Polouvička was about to remind him he had other cars when the door flew open and a fuming Audrey entered the room.

'Richard, you've really done it now, haven't you?' she thundered.

'Well, hello, Audrey,' said the old lady hospitably, but Audrey was obviously in no mood for pleasantries.

'Well, you two young things will want to be alone,' suggested the old lady and diplomatically slipped out of the room.

'What have I done now, Audrey?'

'It seems you've opened my garden to the public.'

'What are you talking about?'

'As I understand it, you've been party to a conspiracy to make my garden a public right of way. Does the name Hartop mean anything to you?'

DeVere thought for a moment.

'Hartop? Oh yes, that funny old archivist from the county library – came here last year to talk about some Pilgrim's Way going through the estate.'

'And you told him that he could re-open an old public right of way through the estate?'

'I know how you feel about tradition.'

'Well, it happens to go right through my garden, and you gave him your permission.'

'Come to think of it, I did. But I didn't know it went through your garden. I thought that path joined up with the Marlbury Road on the other side of the estate.'

'Well, apparently it doesn't. So, to preserve some semblance of privacy, I shall expect you to withdraw your permission forthwith and do everything in your power to keep these people out of my garden.'

With that, she turned and strode from the room, almost flattening Mrs Polouvička, who was listening at the keyhole, as she threw open the door.

'See what I mean?' said the old lady coming back into the room. 'Not my idea of casual.'

Audrey had never really thought of the motor car as a status symbol until this moment. Now, deprived of her Rolls on what seemed at best a semi-permanent basis, she was aware for the first time of the status it gave her – a position in life which she had now lost and that DeVere had attained. The full realization of relative stations was now brought home to her by the sight which confronted her as she left the manor. It was of DeVere's Rolls-Royce parked in the forecourt, being lovingly washed and rubbed down by old Ned.

The concept on which was based the old feudal order which had prevailed at Grantleigh for 400 years was that everybody on the estate knew their place – but the events and upheavals on the Grantleigh estate were gradually calling the whole idea into question. If Audrey could aspire to the level of the lowliest on the estate, it was equally possible that the lowliest could also aspire to the level of the highest, a notion which was now foremost in Ned's mind. It was at times like this when he was cleaning the Rolls that Ned indulged in daydreams about aspiring to the lifestyle of his master. He was thinking that he would give anything to own a motor car like this, and was fantasizing about the possibility of tearing off into the countryside at the wheel and speeding through the country lanes with the roof down, perhaps with a pretty girl at his side.

Audrey's fantasy was less exotic. For her, the transport of the future was the bus.

By the end of the week she'd had her first taste of this primitive form of locomotion. She had chosen the worst possible day for her initiation, since it was market day in the county town. And though that was not the reason she was going there, it accounted for the bus being packed with chattering women and undisciplined children, whom she frequently had to rebuke for rushing from seat to seat.

It was fifteen miles to town by the main road, but the only glimpse she ever caught of the more direct route was when they crossed it every ten minutes or so to pick up more chatterboxes and rioting youngsters at every adjacent village, protracting the journey by another ten miles and an indescribably long time. The only way Audrey could tolerate the indignity of public transport was to suffer in silence, switching off and losing herself in her own thoughts.

At least this was one way of seeing the county, she conceded, as the bus rattled its circuitous way through the country lanes and hamlets. In fact, the experience gave her a high viewpoint of the landscape which she had never seen before from the Rolls, whereby she was able to see over the hedges into rather unsightly tips and wastelands. She began composing angry letters to the council about the shocking state of some of the roadside plots, which she had previously thought of as beauty spots. There was a particularly neglected expanse of rampant brambles on the Marlbury Road which appeared to have been used as a public dump, littered with abandoned cars, pram wheels and the odd bed and armchair.

'Glory be,' she muttered to herself. 'Everything but the . . .' But then she noticed there *was* a kitchen sink.

However, for the moment, she had more important things to think about. Perhaps the thing that ruffled Audrey most about her encounter with the local historian was that she resented being told what's what, or rather, what *used* to be what, by somebody who thought he knew more about the Grantleigh estate than she did. After all she had, in her time, built up a library of books on local history, and indeed had a few of the original old maps of Grantleigh in her possession. While Hartop would have had access to most of the books which were available in the county library, he had not seen the maps and she had looked them out, if not to disprove his routing of the Pilgrims' Way, then at least to verify it. In doing so, she had come across an interesting piece of information which suggested that Hartop might have been wrong and which certainly merited deeper research. It was in the cause of this deeper research that she was now bussing it, old map in hand, to the county library. And so it was that an untypically studious Audrey could be found in the reference library that afternoon. She was fired with a determination to prove that the Pilgrim's Way to Glastonbury did not lead past her compost heap. She did not quite know what she was looking for, but she recognized it when, after a couple of hours of ferreting in the archives, she found it.

'Geronimo!' she jubilated at the top of her voice. Her triumphant outburst drew stern looks from the people at the surrounding desks – bespectacled old men reading periodicals, schoolboys without 'suitable' homes to work in, women looking up their family trees.

'Sshh,' they all cried.

'Don't you shush *me*,' Audrey said defiantly. 'I happen to have made a most significant historical discovery,' she announced.

'Sshh,' came the chorus.

A door to the librarian's office opened and an official bustled out to see what the commotion was all about. It was none other than W. H. Hartop – author of *Somerset Walks*, and an expert on local history.

Audrey could not believe her luck at finding her adversary in scholarship so readily to hand at this moment of truth.

'Just the man I want to see,' she said loudly.

'Sshh,' protested the defenders of silence, and directed Hartop's attention to Audrey.

'Can I help you?' Hartop asked quietly, trying to set a tolerable voice level for the ensuing conversation.

'We met the other day on the Grantleigh estate,' Audrey began.

'Indeed. You live on the Pilgrims' Way, don't you?'

'That's what you think,' she said, dumping a tome in front of him in a cloud of dust.

'Ssshh,' sibilated the chorus, choking on the dust.

'I'd like to know where you got your information from,' she challenged Hartop.

'I assure you, madam, I've researched the whole question very deeply.'

'Then have you read this?' She pointed out a paragraph in the book.

It was an account of the legend of Glastonbury. It explained the origins of the mediaeval pilgrimages instigated by the belief that the chalice used at the Last Supper was buried there by Joseph of Arimathaea. It also went over the evidence that it was at Glastonbury that he made the first British Christian converts. There was also a map to show where the Pilgrims' Way would have gone into what was now the Grantleigh estate and out the other side, although the actual route through the estate was not marked.

'Yes, yes, I've read all this,' said Hartop impatiently.

'Then read it again,' demanded Audrey, pointing out a paragraph.

The legend has it that among the mediaeval monks who made such a pilgrimage was a certain dreamy novice y-clept Brother Matthew who, taking his turn to carry the sacraments, sat down at the side of the road and fell asleep. On waking, he found that the rest of the party had moved on, and in his haste to catch them up, forgot to take the sacraments with him. Realizing this, he returned to the place where he had been asleep and found the spot marked by a shaft of light shining from the sky and the sacraments surrounded by kneeling animals from the neighbouring woods and fields. Conspicuous among them was one creature which was not kneeling – a black sheep.

'Why are you not kneeling?' asked the monk.

'How can you ask such a stupid question,' said the sheep. 'Don't you know who I am?'

'No,' replied the monk.

'I am the Devil.'

'Then why are you in the form of a sheep?'

'I am a sheep because then men may steal me – and then they will be hung and I can have their souls,' explained the Devil.

'Then, in the name of God, begone from this Holy place,' demanded the monk with uncharacteristic temerity. Thereupon the Devil, so astounded at being addressed with such boldness, by such a callow youth, turned and shrank away in shame. This feat of Christian courage was witnessed by some of the other holy pilgrims who had returned in search of their lost brother, and they were so impressed by the holy man's courage in the face of evil that they built a cross to mark the spot where the Devil was vanquished. It was thereafter known as Matthew's Cross.

'Yes, I know the story,' sighed Hartop, looking up.

'But do you know where Matthew's Cross is?'

'Nowhere. It's merely a legend.'

'Is it just?' challenged Audrey, unrolling her ancient map

of Grantleigh. 'What's that, then?' She pointed to a spot just to the west of the Grantleigh boundary. The cross was marked.

'How fascinating,' said Hartop, suddenly put on his metal.

'So answer me this,' demanded Audrey. 'Why would the Pilgrims' Way take a detour of nearly a mile to avoid the cross in order to go through my garden?'

Hartop looked at the map again, taking note of the point where the Pilgrims' Way entered and left the estate.

'If you're right, it means that the Pilgrims' Way would have gone right through Grantleigh Manor itself. Hardly possible.'

'Perfectly possible,' said Audrey. 'Grantleigh Manor wasn't built then.'

Hartop fell silent for a moment.

'Goodness me,' he exclaimed, searching the map again. 'This is certainly news to me,' he admitted humbly. He pointed to the cross. 'What would be on that spot now?'

'It would be somewhere on the Marlbury Road out of the estate. I expect it's somewhere in that derelict bramble patch that the council aren't doing anything about.'

'Do you think the cross could still be there?' asked Hartop.

Audrey realized she had perhaps shown her hand too early.

'I don't know,' she confessed. 'But that is exactly what I intend to find out,' she added, raising her voice to the pitch commensurate with her determination.

'Sshh,' said the chorus of readers.

If there were two people on the Grantleigh estate who fully recognized the importance of casual meetings for the exchange of news, views, confidences or inconsequential chatter, they were Marjory and the rector.

During Audrey's absence at the library, Marjory had

been enjoined to give Bertie his afternoon walk, in the course of which she met the rector.

'Marvellous weather,' said the rector, invoking his usual opening gambit.

'Yes, indeed. Just the thing for good long walks, eh?' agreed Marjory.

'Funny you should mention that,' replied the rector. 'I wonder if you would like to join us for a church social ramble on Saturday?'

'What a wonderful idea,' said Marjory. 'You mean tomorrow?'

'Yes, indeed. Only, I've just been reading the latest edition of *Somerset Walks*, and it appears there is a Pilgrims' Way that leads through the estate, and I thought it would be rather interesting to follow it.'

Marjory suddenly lost her enthusiasm.

'Oh,' she said.

'Do you think Mrs fforbes-Hamilton would like to come?'

'I doubt it somehow.'

'Mr Hartop himself agreed to lead us.'

'Well, I'm not sure if I can make it, rector,' Marjory demurred.

'Oh, do come with us. Everybody else on the estate is coming. Mr Miller has agreed to join us and Mrs Beacham is coming, the brigadier, Ned, Linda, Polly, Mrs Patterson from the shop, and Mr Purvis, and we'll all so miss you.'

Marjory hesitated, but the rector would not be refused.

'And I've even invited Mr DeVere, of course,' he said suggestively. That was all the prompting Marjory needed.

'Oh, very well,' she agreed.

'But alas, Mr DeVere says he can't make it. Still – it should make a very pleasant church outing.'

After her *coup de grâce* in the library, Audrey felt she deserved better than a bus ride back to Grantleigh. But there was no alternative. Soon she was standing in a long bus queue, jostling shoulders with the same unruly travelling companions. She was still there three quarters of an hour later when the bus arrived. She was just about to board it when she caught sight of a Rolls-Royce turning out of the garage next door. She recognized it as DeVere's and, much to the amusement of her fellow queuers, she left the line and ran after it, shouting vociferously.

'Richard, Richard – it's me. Wait.'

But she did not manage to catch the driver's attention and the car was off down the Marlbury Road before she abandoned the chase, by which time, on turning back to the bus station, her bus had gone. It was another half an hour before she was on her way home.

The bus ride home was more agreeable than her inward journey. For one thing, the further it went the emptier and quieter it got. For another thing, there was something to interest her which, as the journey continued, got more and more intriguing. It was the bus's unaccountably frequent encounter with a certain item of traffic – namely, a familiar Rolls-Royce: DeVere's. It seemed that almost every piece of straight road they came to, the same Rolls-Royce overtook them, and at every intersection it crossed their path. The first time it shot by at high speed, Audrey was vaguely aware of somebody sitting in the passenger seat. A girl. A young girl.

It was not until it had overtaken them for the second time and then encountered them again crossing their path at a road junction, that Audrey realized, to her horror, who the girl was. It was Linda Cartwright, the estate groom. Her impression was short lived, because several miles and half an hour later when she saw the car again, it appeared that the girl was not Linda at all but Polly, the gamekeeper's daughter who worked in the Marlbury branch of DeVere's supermarket. Yet half an hour ago it was unmistakably Linda. The car kept appearing – in front of them, behind them, to the left of them, to the right of them. So intrigued did Audrey become, that she kept changing seats in the bus to maximize her view every time the car appeared, much to the consternation or amusement of the few passengers left. Could this be the same woman who had reproached their children that morning for doing much the same thing?

Next time she caught sight of DeVere's Rolls, there appeared to be three more girls in the back of the car, whom, due to the high viewpoint provided by the bus and the speed of the Rolls, Audrey did not have time nor suitable position to identify. But the implications were clear. DeVere had apparently been kerb crawling – ostensibly picking up girls and hell-raising with them all over the countryside at high speed, an impression which was confirmed by her next encounter with the car, nearer to Grantleigh this time, but parked empty in a gateway to a field.

She drew the only conclusion she could. Richard DeVere was practising *doit de seigneur* with any of the estate girls that he might pick up, beguiling them with his flashy car, joy-riding them all over the neighbourhood.

Audrey had heard of strange impulses besetting men at the onset of spring, but this took the biscuit. Well, so much for any casual encounters with him on the highways and byways, she thought. Audrey did not like the company she would be keeping. She was 'not that sort of girl'. Besides, she now had other things to attend to.

Darkness was falling by the time she got back to the lodge, so it was too late for her to go in search of Matthew's Cross now. Nevertheless, she had already had the benefit of a preliminary reconnoitre from the bus.

Taking her bearings from the old map, and taking it that this was the same as the old Marlbury Road, she had little doubt as to the exact location of Matthew's Cross. It would be somewhere in that derelict bramble patch under the old abandoned cars and sinks and beds. She cringed at the prospect of looking for it.

The following morning was taken up with the weekend shopping, but by afternoon she was ready for action and was clad in old clothes, wellingtons and gardening gloves. Brandishing a sickle and the map, she set out to cover the mile or so up the Marlbury Road to the site. She was walking along what she was now certain was the old Pilgrims' Way to institute her assault on the brambles and rubbish in the scrubland the council would do nothing about.

So anxious was she to prove her point, and to do so before Hartop started his own investigations, that she scarcely noticed the distance. It was all in the cause of scholarship.

From ground level the site seemed clearer than it had looked from the bus. There now appeared to be a path through the debris. She followed the channel which led her deeper into the bramble-snarled wood and found herself in a clearing of flattened undergrowth, and there, in a shaft of light shining between the trees, she found it. Without so much as raising a sickle, she had stumbled on a square of stone sticking about a foot out of the ground. It was unquestionably the base of an upturned monument which time had buried in the earth. She felt among the chosen people – after all those centuries, divine providence had selected her as the instrument of this revelation: 'Lead kindly light', she sang as she clawed her way into the ground. She dug away until she saw some decorative carving on a stone stem, then a cross-piece which confirmed that she had found what she was looking for. It was easy, for the earth was loose, almost freshly turned. But to unearth and right the whole structure was more than one person, even of her strength, could manage.

Audrey was beside herself with joy as she left the half-exposed cross and came out of the scrubland back on to the Marlbury Road. She was almost running as she made her way back to the lodge in her enthusiasm to get on the phone to Mr Hartop to report her find. In fact, so keen was she to get back that she was prepared to jettison her principles about accepting charity, and cadge a lift home from the first vehicle that came over the hill. When it came, she hardly heard it steal up behind her. It was not surprising, since it was a Rolls-Roycc, fabled for their silence. And the driver was Richard DeVere. He did not recognize her at first – the woman waving him down was ragged and dirty and bramble-scarred, and as far as he could tell she had just crawled out of a rubbish tip. He drove on past her, swerving slightly, and it was only in the after-image she left him with that he recognized her. He pulled up several yards down the road, turned off the engine and waited for her to catch up.

So much for the chance, off-guard meeting, he thought. She turns up like a tramp for it. But it was undoubtedly her. That was something.

'Audrey, what on earth are you doing here?'

'I've found it, I've found it,' she exulted pointing. 'I must go home at once and phone that idiot Hartop.'

'Can I give you a lift?'

'Quickly, quickly,' she cried, rushing round to the passenger side and getting in. She was lowering her principles thus far – to the extent of riding with the man apparently hell-bent on deflowering every female in the county.

'What on earth are you so steamed up about?' said DeVere.

'The Pilgrims' Way,' she explained. 'It doesn't go through my garden after all. Never did. That cross has been there hundreds of years and nobody knew it. Now, drive on.'

DeVere was not fired by her enthusiasm and seemed in no hurry to have a full explanation. What cross? He sat for a moment and looked at her, drubbing his fingers on the steering wheel.

'Well, if whatever it is has been there for however many hundreds of years, what's the hurry, all of a sudden?'

'I have conclusive proof that the public right of way does not go through my garden.'

'Is that all?' said DeVere unimpressed, and roared with laughter.

Audrey looked at him sternly.

'You can laugh,' she said.

'I am laughing.'

'Yes, but I think you'll find the public right of way goes straight through your house.'

DeVere stopped laughing.

'What are you talking about, Audrey?'

'It's too complicated to explain now. Now, are you going to take me home or not?'

DeVere shrugged his shoulders and pulled the starter. The motor whirred but the engine didn't fire. He turned the ignition key again.

'Come along, Richard,' said Audrey impatiently. 'What's wrong?'

'The car won't start.'

He pulled the starter again, and the engine burst into life for a moment, and then died again. DeVere glanced at the fuel gauge. The needle indicated the petrol tank was empty.

'We're out of petrol,' said DeVere.

'Typical,' sulked Audrey.

'But I can't understand it,' said DeVere scratching his head. 'It was half full yesterday.'

Audrey saw her chance.

'Well, what do you expect if you will gallivant all over the countryside, having your wicked way with all your girl-friends.'

'What are you talking about?'

'Oh, don't act all innocent. I saw you.'

'Saw me doing what?'

'Yesterday. I saw this car at least half a dozen times with a different woman in it every time from what I could see.'

'What are you talking about, Audrey?' said DeVere genuinely mystified. 'This car went in for its service yesterday. I didn't go anywhere in it.'

'But I saw you pick it up from the garage.'

'I didn't pick it up, Ned did.'

'Ned? You mean it was Ned who was gallivanting with those girlfriends all over the place in your car?'

'Must have been. It certainly wasn't me.'

'Well, I never,' sighed Audrey. 'That puts a completely different complexion on things,' she added, settling down and accepting DeVere's innocence in the matter. 'He must have been joy-riding every woman on the estate.'

'Wait till I get my hands on him,' threatened DeVere, looking at the fuel gauge. 'He must have been miles.'

'I'm sorry, Richard, I thought it was you.'

They fell silent for a moment, and then DeVere burst out laughing.

'What's so funny?' Audrey protested. 'It doesn't alter the fact that here we are, stuck in the country lane out of petrol.'

'Exactly,' said DeVere eyeing her suggestively. 'A beautiful day – evening about to fall – and here we are, a man and a woman run out of petrol on a country lane. I feel I'm in a cartoon.'

'Well, what are you going to do about it?' said Audrey, softening.

'Well, what do a man and a woman usually do when they run out of petrol in a country lane?'

Audrey laughed out of embarrassment as much as anything. DeVere looked at her.

'Alone at last,' he said gently, reminding Audrey of Marjory's counsel on the matter of casual meetings.

Alone at last.

They looked at each other tenderly. If something was

going to happen, thought Audrey, it was going to happen now. And something did.

Over the hill came the chatter of voices, heralding a procession of booted and rucksacked ramblers, in fact the parish outing, led by W. H. Hartop who was holding forth.

'And just here is Matthew's Cross which conclusively proves that this is, after all, the old Pilgrims' Way.'

'How fascinating,' said the rector.

'I found it this morning, and I'd be most grateful if you could help me to set it up again.'

'It'll be a pleasure,' cooed Marjory. A refrain of willingness was taken up by the brigadier Mr Miller, Mrs Beacham, Mrs Patterson, Mr Purvis, Linda and Polly. . . .

'Gracious,' said the rector, seeing the Rolls-Royce and its occupants parked at the side of the road. 'And what have we here?'

Audrey and DeVere glowered at the party of ramblers.

'At last, yes,' whispered Audrey to DeVere with disappointment.

'But not alone,' added DeVere mournfully.

7

It was as if fate was intent on punishing Audrey for her presumption. One moment it looked as if she was the chosen one in both scholarship and love, and the next her fantasies lay about her in smithereens. Hers had been the false hopes of a false spring, for at that moment the spring which had brought a scintilla of sunshine into her life declared itself to have been a hoax. The sun went in and wasn't seen again for several weeks. Moreover, not content with just clouding over, the weather seemed to single Grantleigh out for particularly harsh treatment, and the estate was back in the grip of winter.

There is a moment in the midst of every winter when it seems one has entered a new ice age which has no intention of going away. This was it.

Grantleigh certainly could look bleak in the winter – its position in the valley offering scant protection from the elements; only, it seemed, from the light. Broad daylight was so dark sometimes that it took a snow fall to brighten the place up. At least the estate looked picturesque again, even though snow brought much of the farm work to a standstill. At this moment, the weather wasn't doing anything with conviction – Grantleigh appeared to get snow, rain, sleet, hail, thunder and then snow again, all within five minutes. The changeable weather seemed to unsettle the Mideonites whose metabolisms could not keep up, and they began to succumb to their seasonal ailments one after the other.

The first to go down was old Mrs Polouvička, who took to her bed with every conceivable respiratory and muscular malady connected with cold weather, then Brabinger, then Ned, then Mrs Beacham, then Marjory. If this domino-theory were followed through to the bitter end, the last to go down, or so she claimed, would be Audrey. Her boast of having the constitution of an ox, impervious to anything as peripheral as mere weather conditions, was made in a starchy conversation with DeVere one particularly grizzly day after she had visited the ailing Mrs Polouvička.

'Living in the country, you learn to live at one with nature,' Audrey was lecturing as a sheet of sleet tore at the window. You come to know that the weather has its reasons. You'll get acclimatized in a year or ten.'

'It's getting me down, too,' said DeVere gloomily. 'Look, it was snow just now, and now it's sleet. How on earth did you get through the winter months when you lived here?'

'We always went away.'

'Oh, very at one with nature, that,' he jeered.

'All the sensible birds fly south in winter, so why shouldn't we?'

'Where did you go?'

'Zermatt – for the winter sports.'

'Maybe that's what I should do.'

'Oh, do you ski?'

'Of course. I'm rather good, as a matter of fact.'

He looked at the window where the sleet had turned into hail and was now bombarding the window pane.

'Such a wonderful sport,' Audrey went on, against the sound of the rain. 'I learnt as a girl from a rather dishy instructor called Benz.'

'Benz?'

'Oh, it was only a nickname – he used to stand on the hillside all day, shouting "Benzeknees, benzeknees" so we called him Benz.'

She did the action and DeVere imitated her and they

laughed. It was the first laugh they'd had together for days and, unaccountably, it embarrassed them.

'Out on the pistes all day,' sighed Audrey nostalgically, 'that wonderful crispness in the air, the blissful freedom and the smoothing silence of the mountains, the smell of woodsmoke and the *après-ski Apfelstrudel* at "Hans and Gerda's".'

'Yes, and a broken leg.'

'I never broke a leg. I broke an arm oncc, but it was worth it just to have my plaster cast signed by the Aga Khan and Gerald Ford.'

The rain subsided for a moment, but the window pane nearly caved in, buckled by a seering blast of freezing wind which seemed to shake the whole house to its foundations.

'Dear God!' exclaimed DeVere.

'Oh, that reminds me – I've got something for you to sign,' said Audrey, dipping into her handbag and producing a document. 'Parish accounts. I need your authority to buy a new tea-urn for the parish rooms.'

'Ah, good. When are we getting that?'

'Last October. I authorised it verbally, but I need your signature. I'm afraid the parish account is one thing you can't keep in your mother's name.'

DeVere obliged with his signature just as Mrs Beacham came in to announce the arrival of Dr Horton to see the patient upstairs.

'Take him up, would you? And bring him in here for a drink when he's finished,' instructed DeVere.

At the mention of Dr Horton's name, Audrey seemed in a hurry to go.

'Do stay for a drink. You know Horton, don't you?'

'Of course. He's been our family doctor for years, not that I ever needed him with my robust health.'

'What about your husband?'

'Ah, yes, he did treat Marton over his last illness, but I don't hold that against him.'

'Wouldn't you like to renew his acquaintance?'

'No, I'd better not. I had a coffee with him this morning,' she said, affecting indifference, but betraying a hint of some hostility between her and the doctor.

She went to the door, opened it and caught sight of Horton waiting in the hall. She closed the door hurriedly and returned to the centre of the room.

'Could I go out this way?' she asked, pointing to the french window.

DeVere knew better than to question Audrey's irrational behaviour. He noticed that the rain, the hail and the sleet had abruptly stopped, and the wind had dropped, and he could see no reason why she shouldn't go out that way. He opened the french window for her and let her out, registering the sudden mildness in the state of the weather.

'Tch,' he groaned as he shut the french window, 'perishing sun's come out now.'

Audrey's guilty secret which necessitated avoiding Horton at all costs was that she still owed him some money, in fact, for her husband's last treatment. Her little white lie that she had had coffee with him was not particularly serious. No more so, perhaps, than DeVere's to her – that he was a keen skier. In fact, he had never been on skis in his life.

This was a pity, because the keen skier would have had the time of his life on the estate after the following night's heavy snowfall. There was a magnificent run from Windy Ridge to Dingle Bottoms, which Audrey had been known to practise on in the years gone by before going on her winter holiday. In fact, while she was logging that afternoon, the sight of that distant snow-covered hillside at the back of the lodge, put her in mind of those fun-packed winters.

At first she resolved to get the old skis down from the attic and to find her 'snow legs' again. But she thought that skiing out here for any reason other than in preparation for the real thing would be more hurtful than therapeutic.

Anyway, the thought was driven from her mind by Marjory who happened to be passing the lodge.

'Doing your own logs, then?' she asked with nasal unclarity.

'Yes, Brabinger's poorly,' replied Audrey.

'Who isn't in this weather?' said Marjory and sneezed.

'I'm not for one. And what's wrong with you?'

'I've got an awful chill.'

'A chill? No, Marjory, only royalty have chills. What you've got there is a common cold.'

She finished filling the log basket and, as she tried to heave it into the air, one of the handles came off in her hand.

'Oh, drat,' she exclaimed, waving the detached shreds of straw of the basket handle in Marjory's face. 'You see? Even the log basket is in bad shape. Still, you can't expect a cheap souvenir from Morocco to last more than two minutes.'

'When did you get it?' sniffed Marjory.

'Nineteen sixty-two.'

Audrey heaved it on to her shoulder with the remaining handle and straightened up.

'Let me help,' offered Marjory.

'No, no, you're sickening. And Brabinger's ill, so's Ned, so's Mrs Poo, and so is Richard, it seems. In fact, I seem to be the only able-bodied person left on the estate.'

Audrey marched off round to the front door.

'Coming in for a cup of coffee?' she called. 'Or would you prefer a bowl of Friar's Balsam?'

They went into the hall and through to the drawing room where it was Audrey who began sniffing.

'What's that smell?' she said, suddenly aware of something that was bringing tears to her eyes.

'It's the vapour rub on my chest,' admitted Marjory.

'Huh, one of your herbal concoctions, is it?'

'Extract of horse chustnut.'

'I suppose that's better than extract of horse,' Audrey conceded. 'Just don't stand too near the fire or you'll explode. And will you stop sniffing?'

'Can I have a hankey?'

'If you must.'

'Quickly – my nose is running.'

'Well, it's the only thing on this estate that is,' said Audrey putting down the log basket and handing her a box of tissues. 'Honestly, what's wrong with everybody? I'm surrounded by faint hearts and feeble minds,' grumbled Audrey as she heaved the log basket into the air again. 'Am I the only person who's fit around here?'

The basket was suddenly on the ground again, and the sound of straining straw and log-spill was completely drowned by an ear-piercing shriek from Audrey.

'Yaghh!'

Her hands grasped her back and she appeared to be locked in a doubled-up position.

'Whatever's wrong?' exclaimed Marjory, rushing to her assistance.

'My back. It's my back . . . slipped a disc . . .'

The words were strained. She was obviously in agony.

'Get me to the sofa,' she gasped.

All Audrey could utter were yowls and groans as Marjory led her to the sofa and propped her up on a cushion.

'What were you saying about being the only person on this estate who's . . .'

'Oh, never mind,' snapped Audrey, having found a position which offered momentary relief from her pain. 'Call Horton.'

'I'll fetch you some of my knapweed liniment.'

'You won't. I'll have Horton or nothing.'

Marjory went to the phone and looked up the number in Audrey's address book under P for 'private', and dialled, while Audrey continued to moan and wince.

'Are you still a private patient?' asked Marjory, while waiting for the phone to be answered.

'What does it matter? This is an emergency.'

Marjory got through to Dr Horton and explained her dilemma.

'She seems to have done something to her back.'

'I don't *seem* to have done it – I *have* done it,' Audrey corrected.

'Dr Horton wants to know if you can walk.'

'Walk? Of course I can't walk.'

Marjory spoke into the phone again.

'She says she can't walk.'

Audrey wasn't having this discussion going on over her head.

'Let me speak to him,' she said.

'Oh, she's just coming to the phone.'

Audrey heaved herself off the sofa, dropped to the floor and crawled on her hands and knees to the phone.

'Hello, Dr Horton,' she said, turning on the automatic social pilot. 'I'm very well, thank you.'

Marjory sniggered.

'Well, apart from a bad back, that is. . . . No, I've had a *contretemps* with a log basket . . . how long have I had it? Since nineteen sixty-two, I think . . . oh, the back . . . only a minute ago. I'm in absolute agony . . . if you could pop out and have a look . . .'

Her face fell. Horton seemed to be doing more talking than she was.

'Isn't that beside the point? I mean, just because I can crawl to the telephone, it doesn't mean I can walk to the surgery.'

But she didn't have the option.

'I see,' she said, crestfallen, and put down the phone without saying good-bye.

'"If you can walk, evening surgery is at six,"' she echoed, and sniffed. 'Oh, that's all I need,' she said, taking a tissue and blowing her nose. 'I hope I'm not catching a chill.'

Although there was another heavy snowfall which froze *in situ* for several days, Mrs Polouvička was sufficiently recovered to be allowed to spend the days downstairs. This did not please DeVere, as it made her his responsibility. He preferred her upstairs whither he could despatch a minion to deal with her.

She spent the days in the drawing room, and although she didn't say anything or do anything very much, he found her continual presence irritating. The burden of his mother became increasingly heavy as the staff dwindled due to sickness, until eventually he was even having to provide her meals.

'Grub's up,' he announced one evening throwing open the drawing room door and advancing on her with a steaming tray. Her hopes were dashed when she saw what he had brought: a Cavendish Food Television Dinner – still in its tin foil.

'Today's chef's suggestion,' he said.

'Thank you, Bedrich, but I'm ill enough as it is,' said the old lady.

'Nothing wrong with it,' said DeVere. 'If I ask our directors to taste our dog food, the least I can do is to expect my mother to try our TV dinner.'

'You never know what's in these things.'

'It's very wholesome and nourishing. You've got to build your strength up as I want you better by next Saturday.'

It was one of DeVere's old tricks to drop contentious information into conversations casually, as if he were talking about an old and familiar idea. It was the first Mrs Poo had heard of 'next Saturday'.

'Why next Saturday?'

'Because I'm going away for a week, remember?'

She thought it quite possible she had been told and had forgotten.

'Well, business is business,' she said.

'Actually it isn't business – it's a holiday, I'm going skiiing in Switzerland.'

In Mrs Polouvička's book the idea of a holiday for pleasure was equated with sin.

'And leave the business to run itself?' she baulked.

'Of course it can run itself,' he said.

'But you've never been on a pair of skis in your life. You'll break your neck.'

'If Audrey can do it, so can I.'

'Oh, is she going with you? she said, enthusiastically. The idea of Audrey going too appealed to her.

'Um.'

'Do her good to get off the estate. You two spend all your time arguing here.'

DeVere was just about to say that Audrey would not be wanted on the voyage, when a thought struck him with a clangorous 'um'. He toyed with the 'um' for a moment, then turned it over in his mind with evident pleasure, and was soon leaping around the room in great excitement.

'Mother, you're a genius,' he exulted, and kissed her.

'What took you so long to realize that?' she answered mystified.

'That's it!' he went on.

He had realized what it was that lay behind every argument that soured relations between him and Audrey. They were all territorial disputes – they were like two ferocious jungle animals trying to dominate the same territory. It brought out their most aggressive and defensive instincts and left little room for the emergence of other finer feelings. The solution was obvious – remove themselves on to neutral territory, somewhere where their respective domains were not in dispute – where they stood a better chance of being on the same side – Switzerland, for instance.

'Yes, I'm asking Audrey to come with me,' he announced. 'She loves skiing and . . .'

He had seen a snag. Had he not given Audrey the impression he was 'rather good' at skiing? He looked out of the window and saw the solution. Snow. Hillsides covered in the stuff. He'd just have to get some practice in.

'Right,' he said springing into action. 'I'm going to ask her now.'

'Just a moment,' pleaded his mother. She had been doing some thinking, too, and turned huffy. In encouraging their assignations as a general principle she did not intend them to compete with her own demands on her son's affections and attention.

'Huh,' she said, 'I don't see why you should leave me here on my own.'

'I've ordered all my skiing gear and everything, I can't cancel now.'

'Who's going to look after me? Can't you wait until I'm better?'

'You are better.'

'I'm not a hundred per cent fit.'

'You can't expect to be at your age. You're bound to be a bit doddery.'

'A hundred per cent doddery then. Can't you do your skiing here? You've got snow, you've got slopes, you've got hills – what has Switzerland got that this hasn't?'

'*Apfelstrudel* at Hans and Gerda's Restaurant.'

'You want *Apfelstrudel* – I'll make you *Apfelstrudel*.' The conversation was interruped by the phone. DeVere answered it.

It was the Cavendish Travel Office confirming his arrangements.

'No – my requirements have changed. What I want now is a fully serviced chalet – for two – and cancel the ski instructor – I will have learnt by then.'

His mother coughed noisily.

'Look, I think I'd better take this call in the office,' he suggested to spare his mother the pain of overhearing the conversation.

As he put down the phone and was turning towards the door, his mother's coughing fit erupted into a convulsion. If he had not seen this performance before, he would have thought that she was going to die. But even so, there was no doubt that she was making herself ill with the effort of putting on a convincing charade.

'Oh, all right, mother,' DeVere capitulated, 'I'll put it off for a bit.'

He left the room angrily and slammed the door. As soon as the door shut behind him, Mrs Poo recovered, smiled to herself happily, and tucked into her television dinner as if she hadn't eaten for a fortnight.

Anyone who aspires to any kind of elevated lifestyle is well advised to exclude a doctor's surgery waiting room from their social circuit. To the Audreys of this world, they rank in the scale of public places marginally above the rush-hour buses and surburban railway carriages. Not that Audrey had ever seen either, any more than she had seen a waiting room the likes of the one she now entered. Her first glimpse of one, fully populated for evening surgery, put her in mind of Elizabeth Fry visiting Newgate prison. Only this seemed infinitely more germ-ridden; everybody in it was suffering from something, perhaps with the possible exception of the receptionist who was now addressing her.

'Would you like to see the doctor?'

'Of course I would like to see the doctor. I'm not here for my health, you know,' rasped Audrey, leaning heavily on her crummock.

'Do you have an appointment?'

'Certainly. Six o'clock.'

The receptionist consulted her book.

'Well, I can't see it down here.'

'I spoke to Dr Horton personally. Didn't I, Marjory?' she added turning to her companion who was holding her arm.

'Yes, you did.'

'Oh, of course you used to be Mrs fforbes-Hamilton, didn't you?' the receptionist asked her.

Audrey frowned.

'I still am, thank you.'

'Oh yes, Dr Horton did mention it. Said you wanted to register as a National Health patient.'

'I wanted nothing of the sort. I want to see Dr Horton.'

'I'm afraid Dr Horton's panel is full.'

'What does that matter?'

'It means that you will have to sign on with one of the other doctors. Dr Skeffington can take you.'

'Never heard of him.'

'He's new. Only just qualified.'

'No, thank you. I don't want to be a guinea pig.'

'Well, there's Dr Davies.'

'Good heavens, is he still alive?'

'He comes in to help when we're busy.'

'He must be ninety if he's a day. Do you remember him, Marjory?'

'Yes,' said Marjory. 'When I was about six, he came and took out the gardener's boy's tonsils on the kitchen table.'

'I certainly don't want to see *him*,' insisted Audrey. 'Not after what he did to that lovely kitchen table.'

The receptionist held out a large metal tag with a number on it.

'Dr Skeffington it is, then,' she said.

'Whatever's this?' said Audrey taking the sheet of metal and allowing herself to be led to a seat in the room.

'It's your number in the queue,' explained Marjory, a seasoned National Health patient.

'You mean you have to queue? I thought I'd made an appointment.'

'No, you have to wait until your number is called.'

Audrey was furious and indignant.

'So I'm reduced to a number, am I? Honestly, just feel the weight of it. I'm surprised half these people don't die of exhaustion just carrying this to their seats.'

'The weight is so you don't walk off with it,' explained Marjory.

Audrey lowered herself gently into a seat.

'This is too humiliating,' she said. 'We must just hope that nobody sees us. Do you suppose there's anybody here we know?' she asked fearfully.

But that was too much to hope for. Some of the other patients who had availed themselves of newspapers, magazines and comics purely to have something to snigger behind, now lowered them to reveal their identities.

There was old Ned, Mrs Patterson from the village shop, Purvis the postman, Miller the farm foreman, Mrs Beacham and half the domestic staff from the manor.

'Oh, glory, this will be all over the village by the morning,' whispered Audrey when the chorus of 'Hallo Mrs fforbes-Hamilton – fancy seeing you here' had died down.

In seeing Audrey, the other patients appeared to be aware of each other for the first time, and began to enquire after each other's health.

'How are you, Mrs Patterson?'

'Fine thank you, And you, Ned?'

'Fine, Mrs Patterson, thank you.'

'How's things, Mr Purvis?'

'Fine thank you, Mrs Beecham.'

'Mr Purvis?'

'Fine, thank you. And you, Miller?'

'Fine, thank you. And you, Ned?'

'Fine.'

'Fine.'

'Fine.'

Audrey looked bewildered.

'Well, if everybody is so well, what are they all doing here?' she asked.

The receptionist had been engaged in an animated telephone conversation, and now replaced the receiver and addressed the waiting room at large from her hatch.

'Can I have your attention please everybody? I'm afraid Dr Skeffington is ill.'

'I'm not surprised, working in a place like this,' whispered Audrey. 'Everybody spreading germs like a Morris Dancer's hankey.'

The receptionist continued.

'So some of Dr Skeffington's patients will have to see Dr Horton . . .'

'Ah, good,' said Audrey very relieved. 'If they'd let me see Dr Horton in the first place it would have saved Dr Skeffington the trouble of being ill.' The receptionist continued her reallocations.

'Those Dr Skeffington patients with numbers one to ten – the rest will see Dr Davies.'

Audrey looked at her number tag. It was number eleven.

Audrey had underestimated the local people in thinking that she only had to wait until the following morning for news of her indisposition to travel round the estate. In fact, it got back to the estate before she did. She'd hardly returned from the doctor's and settled herself down on the sofa to begin her convalescence when she had her first visitor. Marjory, answering the door, gave Audrey a chance to throw the infusion of marigold tea which she had made for her into one of the flower pots. Marjory's instructions had been to get rid of the visitor, but the rising noise level in the hall indicated that she had been unsuccessful. Recognizing the visitor's voice, Audrey scrambled to make herself presentable, achieving virtually nothing before DeVere was in the room.

'And how's the invalid?' he said.

'I'm not an invalid,' replied Audrey coldly.

'I've brought you some flowers.'

'He handed over some daffodils.

'Why, thank you,' she said, admiring them. 'How lovely. Grantleigh's?'

'No. We get them from Jersey.'

He presented her with a box of chocolates.

'You shouldn't have,' she said, taking them and turning the box over and reading the inscription 'Cavendish Selection, Sample Only'.

'I didn't have much time to get anything special,' he said.

'It's certainly a lot better than marigold tea.'

'What's that?'

'One of Marjory's herbal remedies.'

'Oh, you're not putting your trust in that sort of nonsense, are you?'

'No, of course not. Next she'll be telling me that the only way to cure my back is to face north and spit three times on a frog.'

'Why don't you send for Dr Horton?' he suggested.

'Because . . .' she faltered. Let it not be said that Dr Horton had refused to see her, or why.

'Well, I don't send for the doctor just for a bit of backache.'

'Oh, is that all it is?' he asked with concern.

'Yes, that's all.'

'Even so, I think you should get him to look at you. I'll give him a ring.'

Audrey lurched over on the sofa to prevent him getting near the phone.

'No, Richard,' she intervened at the cost of a stab of pain.

'Are you sure?'

'Quite sure. There's absolutely nothing that any doctor can do with backache. I wouldn't dream of wasting his time.'

DeVere relented.

'All right.'

The conversation flagged for a moment.

'Oh, by the way,' said DeVere. 'I was thinking of going on a skiing holiday.'

'How lovely.'

'But I've postponed it.'

'Why?'

'Well, with me away – and your back – the estate would grind to a halt, wouldn't it?'

'That's very thoughtful of you, Richard. As a matter of fact, I've been terrified to think what people might get up to the minute my back is cricked.'

'We must have you better soon. When you're fit I have a proposition to put to you. In fact, I insist on letting the doctor see you.'

'No, really. I wouldn't go near one.'

Marjory came in, bearing a tea tray.

'Audrey, you are naughty,' she said. 'Guess what I've just found in your overcoat pocket?'

She was holding up a metal surgery tag, with the number eleven on it.

'Your surgery number.'

DeVere continued to visit Audrey regularly over the next few days. His visits to the sick-bed were formal – those of a touring minister of health rather than those of a ministering angel. He did not use the occasions to declare himself; that would come later – on neutral ground.

Now that her son had agreed to postpone his holiday, Mrs Polouvička could relax again – and relax she did, sleeping most of the time on the sofa, mostly oblivious of anything that DeVere happened to be doing. She had certainly forgotten all about the skiing trip.

She was therefore rather startled one afternoon a few days later to wake up and see her son rocking back and forth behind the sofa, clothed in white and apparently defying the law of gravity. For a moment she mistook him for an angel and thought that her time had come. But then she realized he was repeating some incomprehensible mantra or litany.

'Benzeknees, benzeknees, benzeknees,' he was intoning.

Her second thought was that he must have joined some transcendental religion. She would have had to have many more thoughts before arriving at the truth, since the explanation was just as unlikely – that DeVere was swaying back and forth on skis in his new ski suit.

'What on earth are you doing, Bedrich?'

'My skiing gear has just arrived.'

She stared at the suit, the bobble hat and the goggles in disbelief.

'You look ridiculous.'

'Can't you see me on the slopes next week, schussing down the Matterhorn?' he said, picking up the new technical term from a book of instructions.

'Well, you can schuss here.'

'Mother, I've got to go skiing some time, otherwise it'll be me who drops dead, as well as you.'

'Then it'll be a very nice family occasion. You cannot leave your sick mother to look after herself.'

'The doctor said that you were perfectly all right. What's more, you're costing me a fortune in doctor's bills, flowers and chocolates.'

Mrs Poo rose to the bait.

'Me?' she said suggestively. 'Or Audrey – you spend most of your time down at the lodge with her. Every afternoon, in fact.'

'I've never known you complain of my spending time with her before,' he said, knowing that this argument had to be seen through, and shuffling round on his skis to face her.

'I'm not complaining. It's just that you seem to be seeing so much of her here, so what is the point of going away?'

'Because . . .' started DeVere. But his mother wouldn't understand the territorial imperative. 'Anyway, I'm not in a hurry for her to recover.'

'Why not?'

'Because the longer she's on her back, the more skiing practice I can get in. I can't have her slaloming down the black runs with me on the nursery slopes, can I?' he added, tossing off the technical terms as if he hadn't just got them out of *Teach Yourself Skiing*.

'Well, please yourself,' said his mother. 'But don't let too much time go by.'

'All right – I'll ask her this afternoon,' said DeVere.

'Good boy – you know what they say? "There is no music played until the bow and the fiddle are together".'

DeVere hadn't heard this one before.

'Is that an old Czechoslovakian saying?'

'No. I just made it up.'

That afternoon, as she was passing the lodge, Marjory experienced an optical illusion. She saw a figure at the back of the house bearing a log basket from the shed into the back door. There was nothing strange about that, except that the figure was strangely like Audrey. It could not have been because Audrey's condition had lately taken a turn for the worse and she had been unable to leave the sofa. She had been groaning in pain the day before, and suffered a relapse when DeVere came round bearing more flowers and chocolates for her, so it was impossible that she could have recovered this quickly.

But it must have been an illusion, because when she entered the lodge she found Audrey lying on the sofa, apparently unable to move. Yet the fire was blazing and the log basket was full.

'How are you today then?' Marjory asked.

'A little better, thank you, but I think it'll be a long haul yet.'

Marjory described her hallucination, but Audrey made her none the wiser.

'What do you expect if you will drink that marigold tea of yours,' she said.

'Then who did I see?' Marjory said.

'It was probably Brabinger.'

'In a coat and skirt?'

'Well, it is his day off.'

'I could have sworn it was you. Are you sure you were in here all the time?'

Audrey sighed a 'how-many-times-do-I-have-to-tell-you' sigh.

'Marjory, for the last few days I've been totally unable to move, and you know that it has been my practice, though I wish it were different, to have a nap in the afternoons – and today I have had a very good one.'

As Audrey drew her rug around herself, Marjory caught sight of incriminating evidence, and turned back the end of the rug.

Audrey was wearing boots.

'In your wellingtons?' she asked.

Audrey looked at her muddy footwear as if she had never seen them before. She knew that she could not explain them away.

'Oh, all right, it *was* me you saw.'

'So, you've recovered?'

'Well, if you must know, yes. Yes, I have. I've felt perfectly all right since Saturday.'

'Then why are you still lying around? It's not like you.'

'I have my reasons.'

'Oh, is one of them called Richard DeVere?'

'You're very nosy, Marjory, but if you must know, it's also all the others.'

So that was it. There had been nothing wrong with Audrey for the last few days, yet she had purposely prolonged her incapacity.

'I'm sure that if you had the opportunity, you'd do the same. I'm an ordinary woman, Marjory, and I like being visited every day by a gentleman who brings me chocolates and flowers and presents.'

'And the minute you get better, he'll stop coming, is that it?'

'Yes, I think that's the situation.'

Audrey's reasoning was sometimes beyond telling, thought Marjory. But her discovery of the deception had put her at an advantage which she was not going to let slip.

'Honestly, you are inconsistent, Audrey. Only the day before yesterday you were complaining of the indignity of entertaining a gentleman on your back.'

Audrey had obviously rationalized that as well. She whirled her arm about her head with a triumphant flourish.

'*La couchée et la levée de la reine*.' she declaimed dramatically.

'I beg your pardon?' said Marjory.

'The getting up and the going to bed of the queen,' Audrey translated. 'The tradition practised by royal households of Europe in the sixteenth century until quite recently. And if receiving people in bed is good enough for the kings and queens of England, then it's good enough for me,' she said, and disported herself in the noblest posture she could manage at the horizontal.

The door bell rang.

'If that's Richard, not a word.'

Marjory went out into the hall to open the door. Audrey slipped off her wellingtons and re-posed herself in her *tableau vivant*. She heard the voices in the hall, and whoops of admiration from Marjory.

'How's the patient?' asked DeVere.

'It's time for her *levée*,' said Marjory.

'Then I'll wait until she's finished,' replied DeVere.

'No, no, please go through. I'll go and make some tea.'

By the time he was in the drawing room, Audrey had composed herself to give the impression that she was anxious not to show that she was in pain. Her half-closed eyes opened wide at the sight of DeVere. He was dressed in his white ski suite.

'How are we today?' he asked.

'Still suffering, I'm afraid.'

'I'm sorry to hear that.'

'What are you dressed like that for?'

'I was just going to put in some skiing practice – I'm a bit rusty. . . . How long do you think it's going to be before you're on your feet?'

'I'm afraid it may be some time,' said Audrey, as if a spasm of pain had racked her body.

'You're not likely to recover in, say, the next couple of weeks?' said DeVere.

'Ah, I wish it were possible,' sighed Audrey.

'That's a pity. I'll just have to forget it.'

'Forget what?'

'Well, you see I'm going away. My skiing holiday.'

'Oh, so you won't be coming to see me?'

'Well, it wasn't so much that – I was wondering if you'd like to come with me.'

Audrey sat bolt upright, forgetting to register pain.

'Oh, Richard,' she said with alarm, and then sank back as if to cover her tracks, 'how kind.'

'However,' said DeVere shaking his head, 'since you're in such a bad state, it's clearly out of the question for quite a while.'

There was no sign of pain now – it was adrenalin pounding through her body as she began to think very fast.

'But if I were, say to recover . . . ?'

'You said there wasn't any chance of that.'

Audrey had her answer ready.

'Marjory has some wonderful herbal cures, noted for their quck results.'

'Well, let's hope for a miracle. But there's no hurry – soon as you're ready.'

The door opened and Marjory came in with a tea tray.

She poured a cup for Audrey. Audrey sipped it and all but spat it out again.

'Marjory, what on earth have you put in this?'

'Nothing,' stammered Marjory, bewildered. 'You told me not to.'

'No, I didn't,' Audrey lied. 'I don't like your miracle cures, but no doubt this tannis root or whatever it is will do me the power of good. I shall expect quick results, Marjory.'

In the attic of the old lodge, there was a skylight which commanded a good view of the ski-run from Windy Ridge down to Dingle Bottoms, the lower slopes of which could not be seen from the lodge at ground level. Although it was perilously close to the lodge, DeVere felt that he was safe to practise his skiing in the dip without being seen.

He was not to know that the moment he was out of the house, Audrey had leapt from her sick-bed and skipped upstairs to the attic to look out her skiing things, which had not seen the light of day since she had left the manor. DeVere was not aware that from the attic he could be seen as he shuffled across the snow to where Ned was waiting with a tractor and winch. He had already had a few runs on the gentler slopes with Ned winching him up and then letting him down slowly on a cable, but he did not yet feel confident enought to entrust himself to the laws of gravity.

'Benzeknees, benzeknees,' he kept saying to himself as he tried to relax on his skis.

As his confidence grew, Ned took the tractor further and further up the slope until DeVere was having such a good time that he forgot that he might be seen, and allowed the tractor to take him to start the run at the brow of the hill.

'Well, I think it's a dirty trick,' Marjory said as they passed various items of junk between them in the attic, so that they could get at the skis.

'I'm going with him and you can't dissuade me,' said

Audrey emphatically.

'But . . .'

'Marjory, I'm going up the Matterhorn and that's flat.'

Marjory accepted it.

'And I'd love to see his face when I tell him I'm coming,' said Audrey, glancing out of the little window. 'What on earth . . . ?' She focused her eyes on the distant figures on the crest of Windy Ridge.

'Look,' she said. 'It's Richard and Ned, and I do believe . . .'

She clambered over the attic debris, slipped through the hole in the floor, and down the ladder, and raced down to the drawing room, grabbing her binoculars from their place under the sofa cushions. She rushed outside.

By the time Marjory had caught her up, Audrey had already seen everything she needed to see.

'I thought so,' she said. 'He's as stiff as a ramrod, and he's standing all wrong.'

'I thought he told you he was a good skier,' said Marjory.

'Skier? Absolute horse feathers! He can't have been on skis in his life. Just look at him.'

She handed Marjory the binoculars.

'Oh, yes. Ned's letting him down on a winch.' They had a clear picture of DeVere gingerly slithering down the slope as the winch paid him out, slowly, and obviously concentrating very hard on staying upright. The two women roared with laughter.

'Oh, I am going to enjoy this,' said Audrey. 'It means when we get to Switzerland, I'm going to have to teach him. I'm going to have the time of my life!'

Halfway down the slope, DeVere was obscured by a foreground ridge, so they did not see what happened next.

The winch cable on the back of Ned's tractor had been long enough to reach the bottom of the slope when he started halfway down, but not now he was on the top of the hill. On one end was DeVere. At the other end there had been nothing but its own pull to give it purchase on its drum. The cable ended and just slipped away, and suddenly DeVere, with several hundred yards of clear slope in front of him, was flying solo. With nothing to hold him back, he accelerated fast. Miraculously, he stayed upright as he came to the bottom and into the dip, but he had not learnt how to stop. His momentum carried him forward towards the brow of the smaller hill, over the top and out of sight and – just as well in view of what he was shouting – out of earshot. Ned had a grandstand view of this spectacle from the seat of his tractor. Over the brow of that hill it was a sheer drop down to Miller's poultry sheds, mused Ned, mentally mapping out DeVere's itinerary. A crash of splintering timbers and a loud squawking indicated that DeVere and the chickens were already getting acquainted.

The following afternoon, Audrey felt she had allowed decent time for Marjory's miracle cure to take effect. She was emboldened to go across to the manor to announce her recovery and her intention to take DeVere up on his invitation.

The sun was shining, the snow was thawing, and snowdrops and crocuses were peeking through, as if Audrey needed evidence that, after all, God was in His heaven – and all was well with her little world.

She was let into the manor by Mrs Polouvička, who had also rallied from her indisposition and seemed in surprisingly good spirits.

'How lovely to see you looking so well again,' said Audrey.

'And you, too. On your feet again so soon?' said the old lady.

'It was Marjory's herbal remedy which finally did the trick. I should bear that in mind if you ever have a bad back. Is Richard in?'

'Yes, he is.'

'I expect he's very busy getting business out of the way ready for his holiday, but I would like to see him.'

'Oh, do go in,' said the old lady pointing to the drawing room door. 'He'll be very pleased to see you.'

Audrey walked into the drawing room where it seemed to be business as usual. DeVere was sitting behind the desk working in his city suit, and did not get up to greet her.

'Audrey,' he said. 'That was a quick recovery.'

'Marjory's little miracle worker. I'm now as fit as a flea, and raring to go.'

She gave him her skiing pantomime – 'Benzeknees, benzeknees,' she laughed.

He looked at her sympathetically. It did not seem that he was as raring to go as she was.

'I'm very pleased to see you, Audrey, of course, but . . .'

'Of course, so that you can whisk me off to the snowy slopes of Switzerland with cries of "*Vive le sport*".'

'Well, not exactly. I just wanted you to sign something.'

Audrey took a pen from her handbag.

'Of course,' she said. 'Business before pleasure. The parish minutes, is it?'

'No,' said DeVere. 'This.'

He pushed back his swivel chair and heaved a plaster cast encasing his left leg on to the desk.

'Sorry, Audrey,' he said, sensing her dismay. 'Holiday's off. I couldn't benz zis knee if I tried.'

She signed away her hopes and dreams with a heavy heart.

DIARY OF A SOMEBODY
Christopher Matthew

'Quite definitely the funniest book I've had the pleasure of reading.' *Tribune*

At weekend houseparties and the elegant gatherings of the London season, at trendy Workers' Workshops and in the expectant crowds at the new National, Simon Crisp is always noticed. He's the one with the coffee stains on his trousers, the air of punctured dignity and educated worry. Humiliated by hurled apple cores and exploding plastic pants, by practical jokes in the office and in his West London flat, he's a fall-guy for our times.

This is his diary. It curiously resembles that classic of ninety years ago, *The Diary of a Nobody*. Especially in one respect: Simon never sees the joke.

But we do. And deliciously so.

'A genuinely funny book.' *Benny Green, Spectator*

'Spellbinding. I read the diary in one sitting.' *The Times*

90p

1941

Bob Gale

Six days after Pearl Harbour, a Japanese submarine surfaces off the coast of California. Its mission – to capture Hollywood. . . . The result – total unbridled lunacy!

Now an outrageous new film from Steven Spielberg – director of *Jaws* and *Close Encounters of the Third Kind, 1941* is a comedy of errors on the grand scale.

£1·00

A LITTLE ZIT ON THE SIDE

Jasper Carrott

He's been a delivery boy (the terror of Solihull), a toothpaste salesman (for four hours), a folkie (repertoire – two songs) – and the most unlikely and original comic superstar for years.

Now Jasper Carrott reveals more of the outrageous talent that has taken him from the Boggery to a series of one-man shows that won him ITV's Personality of the Year Award.

Discover the do-it-yourself man, how to become star of Top of the Pops and the Carrott guide to dog-training. Relive the simple pleasures of The Magic Roundabout, Funky Moped and the Mole.

85p